PAUL TEMPLE AND THE CANTERBURY CASE

Francis Durbridge

WILLIAMS & WHITING

Cover design by Timo Schroeder

9781915887269

Williams & Whiting (Publishers)
15 Chestnut Grove, Hurstpierpoint,
West Sussex, BN6 9SS

Titles by Francis Durbridge published by Williams & Whiting

1   The Scarf – tv serial
2   Paul Temple and the Curzon Case - radio serial
3   La Boutique – radio serial
4   The Broken Horseshoe – tv serial
5   Three Plays for Radio Volume 1
6   Send for Paul Temple – radio serial
7   A Time of Day – tv serial
8   Death Comes to The Hibiscus – stage play
    The Essential Heart – radio play
    (writing as Nicholas Vane)
9   Send for Paul Temple – stage play
10 The Teckman Biography – tv serial
11 Paul Temple and Steve – radio serial
12 Twenty Minutes From Rome – a teleplay
13 Portrait of Alison – tv serial
14 Paul Temple: Two Plays for Radio Volume 1
15 Three Plays for Radio Volume 2
16 The Other Man – tv serial
17 Paul Temple and the Spencer Affair – radio serial
18 Step In The Dark – film script
19 My Friend Charles – tv serial
20 A Case For Paul Temple – radio serial
21 Murder In The Media – more rediscovered serials and
    stories
22 The Desperate People – tv serial
23 Paul Temple: Two Plays for Television
24 And Anthony Sherwood Laughed – radio series
25 The World of Tim Frazer – tv serial
26 Paul Temple Intervenes – radio serial
27 Passport To Danger! – radio serial
28 Bat Out of Hell – tv serial
29 Send For Paul Temple Again – radio serial

60 Paul Temple and the Alex Affair – radio serial
61 Kind Regards From Mr Brix – a novel

Murder At The Weekend – the rediscovered newspaper
serials and short stories

Also published by Williams & Whiting:

Francis Durbridge: The Complete Guide
By Melvyn Barnes

Titles by Francis Durbridge to be published by Williams &
Whiting
Paul Temple: Two Plays For Radio Vol 2 (Send For Paul
Temple and News of Paul Temple)
They Knew Too Much – magazine serial
The Yellow Windmill – magazine serial (extended version)

INTRODUCTION

Francis Durbridge (1912-98) was a prolific writer of sketches, stories and plays for BBC radio from 1933. At first they were mainly light entertainments, including libretti for musical comedies, but a talent for crime fiction became evident in his early radio plays *Murder in the Midlands* (1934) and *Murder in the Embassy* (1937). The *Radio Times* (11 February 1938) mentioned that Durbridge had by then written some one hundred radio pieces, and Charles Hatton commented in *Radio Pictorial* (28 October 1938) that "He is one of the very few people in this country who have succeeded in making a living by writing for the BBC."

A significant year for Durbridge was 1938, when he created the novelist/detective Paul Temple and his wife Steve. *Send for Paul Temple* was broadcast from 8 April to 27 May 1938 in eight twenty-five minute episodes and attracted over 7,000 fan letters, thus ensuring that the Temples were securely launched. The result was a succession of twenty more Temple cases, from *Paul Temple and the Front Page Men* (1938) to *Paul Temple and the Geneva Mystery* (1965), plus new productions of some of the serials.

In the mid-twentieth century radio detectives were extremely popular, and Temple's rivals included Dick Barton (by Edward J. Mason), Philip Odell (by Lester Powell), Dr Morelle (by Ernest Dudley), PC 49 (by Alan Stranks) and Ambrose West (by Philip Levene). And beyond the UK the Paul Temple serials acquired an enormous following, with translated versions broadcast in the Netherlands from 1939, Germany from 1949, Italy from 1953 and Denmark from 1954.

This volume, *Paul Temple and the Canterbury Case*, publishes the cinema spin-off of the fifth Paul Temple radio serial *Send for Paul Temple Again*, which was broadcast from

13 September to 1 November 1945 in eight thirty-minute episodes. The original radio serial marked the appearance of Marjorie Westbury (1905-89) as Steve Temple on the first of twenty-two occasions. Playing opposite, for his only time as Temple, was the London-born Canadian actor Barry Morse (1918-2008), who also appeared the following year in Durbridge's radio play *The Caspary Affair*. Then much later Morse achieved international stardom on television as the dogged Lt Gerard in pursuit of Dr Richard Kimble (played by David Janssen) in *The Fugitive* from 1963 to 1967.

Send for Paul Temple Again was broadcast soon after in the Netherlands, with the Dutch radio version *Haal Paul Vlaanderen er weer bij!* (17 February – 7 April 1946, eight episodes) translated by J.C. van der Horst and produced by Kommer Kleijn, starring Jan van Ees as Vlaanderen and Eva Janssen as Ina. Then in April 1948 John Long published it as a novel, written jointly by Durbridge and Charles Hatton, which appeared in translation in Germany as *Paul Temple jagt Rex*, in France as *L'insaisissable Rex*, in the Netherlands as *Paul Vlaanderen trekt van leer*, in Spain as *Scotland Yard llama a Paul Temple* and in Sweden as *Paul Temple kommer igen*. And much later a UK audiobook was marketed on audiocassettes and CDs, read by Peter Wickham (ISIS Audiobooks, 2008).

The cinema version of *Send for Paul Temple Again* was released by Butchers/Nettlefold in 1948 under the title *Calling Paul Temple*. The first working title was *Paul Temple and the Canterbury Case* (hence that of Durbridge's screenplay in this volume), which then became the prosaic *Paul Temple – 999* before finally (as *Calling Paul Temple*) the screenplay was not only credited to Durbridge but also to A.R. Rawlinson and Kathleen Butler. Produced by Ernest G. Roy and directed by Maclean Rogers, the film was shown in Germany and Austria as *Wer ist Rex?* and in Sweden as

Kvinnan i grått. It was marketed on DVD by Renown Pictures in 2009, and also included in their DVD box set of all four Temple films as *The Paul Temple Collection Limited Edition* (Renown Pictures, 2011). Most recently, *Calling Paul Temple* was revived on one DVD containing the English and German (dubbed) versions entitled *Wer ist Rex?* (Pidax, 2015).

For those interested in all four cinema films featuring Paul Temple, some information might be useful here. Firstly, *Send for Paul Temple* (Butchers/Nettlefold, 1946) was based on Durbridge's 1938 radio serial of the same name, with a screenplay by John Argyle and Durbridge, produced/directed by Argyle and starring Anthony Hulme and Joy Shelton. Next came *Calling Paul Temple*, as mentioned above, starring John Bentley and Dinah Sheridan. Thirdly, *Paul Temple's Triumph* (Butchers/Nettlefold, 1950) was based on Durbridge's 1939 radio serial *News of Paul Temple*, with a screenplay by A.R. Rawlinson, produced by Ernest G. Roy and directed by Maclean Rogers, and again starring Bentley and Sheridan. And finally, *Paul Temple Returns* (Butchers/Nettlefold, 1952) was based on Durbridge's 1942 radio serial *Paul Temple Intervenes*, with a screenplay by Durbridge, produced by Ernest G. Roy and directed by Maclean Rogers, but this time pairing Bentley with Patricia Dainton.

To complete the history of the 1945 radio serial *Send for Paul Temple Again*, it received a new lease of life over twenty years later when Durbridge was being pressed for a new Temple serial to follow *Paul Temple and the Geneva Mystery* (1965). Although he relented to some extent, he was heavily involved with his television work and this probably explains why *Paul Temple and the Alex Affair* (26 February to 21 March 1968) was a revised and updated production of *Send for Paul Temple Again* rather than an entirely new serial. It had new episode titles, changes in structure and dialogue, and a villain called Alex rather than Rex.

Although no recording of the 1945 serial *Send for Paul Temple Again* has survived, Durbridge's original script has now been published by Williams & Whiting. And in its later radio manifestation, audiocassettes and CDs of *Paul Temple and the Alex Affair* were marketed by BBC Audio in 2003 and later included in the CD set *Paul Temple : The Complete Radio Collection: The Sixties 1960-1968* (BBC, 2017).

Melvyn Barnes
Author of *Francis Durbridge: The Complete Guide* (Williams & Whiting, 2018)

PAUL TEMPLE
AND THE CANTERBURY CASE
A film script
By FRANCIS DURBRIDGE
filmed as
CALLING PAUL TEMPLE
Based on the serial
SEND FOR PAUL TEMPLE AGAIN
CAST:

Paul Temple	John Bentley
Steve Temple	Dinah Sheridan
Mrs Barbara Trevelyan	Margaretta Scott
Dr Charles Kohima	Abraham Sofaer
Norma Rice	Celia Lipton
Sir Graham Forbes	Jack Raine
Edward Latham	Alan Wheatley
Wilfred Davies	Hugh Pryse
Leo Brent	John McLaren
Frank Chester	Michael Golden
Inspector Crane	Ian MacLean
Rikki	Shaym Bahadur
Millie	Merle Tottenham
Carol Reagan	Mary Midwinter
Spider Williams	Wally Patch
Waiter at The Falcon Inn	Aubrey Mallalieu
Doctor	Hugh Miller
Ivy (Girl in Boat)	Maureen Glynne
Maitre d'Hotel	Paul Sheridan
Ticket Inspector	George Merritt
Boatman	Harry Herbert
Bert (Boy in Boat)	Gerald Rex
Esther Van Ralston	Marion Taylor
Pianist	Steve Race
Passer-by	Michael Ward

OPEN TO: The Main and Credit Titles are superimposed
            on a picturesque long shot of Canterbury. If
            necessary, several different views may be used
            dissolving one to the other as the various titles
            dissolve – the final lettering fading out just
            ahead of the last picture and leaving us with an
            impression of the great tower of the Cathedral
            brooding over the city.

We FADE OUT:

CUT TO: A library of location shots of some Kent
Landscape. Night.
The Canterbury-London Express Train is speeding past.
Smoke fills the screen.

CUT TO: The Train Corridor. Night.
Smoke comes in from an open window in the corridor.
A TICKET INSPECTOR comes out of a compartment, sees
the smoke coming in and closes the window.
As he does so a man (FRANK CHESTER) passes behind him
down the corridor.
We do not see his face clearly, though he stops for a moment
to light a cigarette for a girl passenger who is standing in the
corridor.
He is wearing gloves.
The TICKET INSPECTOR goes into the next compartment.

CUT TO: 1st Compartment. Night.
WILFRED DAVIES is alone in the compartment.
He is engrossed in a book.
He is a quick speaking, little Welshman.
A commercial traveller.
The TICKET COLLECTOR enters.

1

INSPECTOR: Ticket, please.

Without looking up, DAVIES hands the INSPECTOR a ticket.
The INSPECTOR looks at it.
We see that DAVIES has actually handed the INSPECTOR a
visiting card which reads:
MR WILFRED DAVIES
The QUICK-BOIL KETTLE CO, LTD.
Pontypool,
S. Wales.

INSPECTOR: Very useful in the home, sir. But what you
             need in a train is your ticket.

DAVIES looks up, takes back the card and smiles
apologetically.

DAVIES: Lordy, man! I'm sorry.

DAVIES finds his railway ticket and hands it to the
INSPECTOR who clips it and hands it back.

INSPECTOR: Thank you, sir. Now you can enjoy your
             thriller in peace.

The INSPECTOR goes out of the compartment while DAVIES
once more becomes immersed in his book.

CUT TO: The Train Corridor. Night.

Smoke is again coming in through the corridor window which
has slipped down.
With a muttered imprecation the INSPECTOR pulls it up. As
the glass windowpane rises, we see reflected in it the next
compartment with a woman seated in the corner, apparently
asleep in a curious slumped attitude.
A sufficient quantity of smoke must be passing the window to
blot out the countryside beyond unless BACK PROJECTION
is used.
THE INSPECTOR glances at the reflection for a moment,
then seeing that the window is secure enters the 2nd
compartment.

CUT TO: The 2nd Compartment. Night.

The INSPECTOR comes in from the corridor.

The WOMAN doesn't move.

INSPECTOR: Ticket, please.

The WOMAN remains motionless.

INSPECTOR: (*Louder*) Ticket, please, madam.

There is still no response.

The INSPECTOR puts his hand on the WOMAN's shoulder to wake her, whereupon she slumps forward and sideways, and we see a knife sticking in her back.

She then falls about the seat.

An expression of horror comes over the INSPECTOR's face, but his exclamation is drowned by the shrill whistle of the engine and a deafening clatter as the train enters a tunnel.

The INSPECTOR rushes out of the compartment.

The rolling of the train causes the WOMAN's body to rock gently to and fro – her arm swinging.

The clatter of the wheels continues.

CUT TO: The Train Corridor. Night.

The INSPECTOR is just coming from the 1st compartment followed by DAVIES whom he has obviously summoned for assistance.

DAVIES, hastily called, is still carrying his book.

The lights of a signal-box flare past as the train leaves the tunnel and the clatter dies.

The INSPECTOR and DAVIES enter the 2nd compartment.

CUT TO: The 2nd Compartment. Night.

The INSPECTOR and DAVIES hurry in.

The WOMAN is still lying sideways on the seat, the knife in full view.

The cessation of the clattering enhances the eeriness as the two men stand looking down at the body.

Then DAVIES bends down and examines the WOMAN's eyelid, putting his book down on the opposite seat.

DAVIES: She's dead, man. What are you going to do? Pull the communication cord?

INSPECTOR: That won't help now – only hang up the train. I'll see if there's a doctor with us. Would you wait here, sir? And don't let anyone in.

DAVIES: Better put the blinds down.

The INSPECTOR pulls down one of the compartment blinds. Scrawled across it roughly in chalk are the letters REX.

DAVIES: (*Intrigued; mutters:*) REX.

The camera pans to the seat where the thriller DAVIES has been reading lies open.

We read the title page:

THE MONOGRAM MURDERS

by

PAUL TEMPLE

Published for The Detective Club

by Collins

14, St James Place,

London.

CUT TO:The Temples' London Flat. Bedroom. Night.

The Temples' London Flat is a composite set comprising a Sitting Room, Bedroom, Kitchen, Bathroom, all opening off a small square hall from which the front door leads on to the landing outside.

From the book in the train, we DISSOLVE into a bedside table upon which are a number of Paul Temple books, enclosed between bookends.

Titles might be "The Kowferry Case", "Enter Carl Hoffman", "Death at Elders End", "Inspector McNair Returns", "The Owl House", etc.

All are by PAUL TEMPLE.

We see the reflection of TEMPLE himself in the dressing table mirror.

He is feverishly tying an evening tie.

He is in shirt-sleeves and calls (or rather his reflection does!)

TEMPLE: Steve! Steve!

STEVE TEMPLE comes into the room from the Hall.

She is in an evening dress and carrying her evening bag and cloak.

STEVE: What's the matter, darling?

TEMPLE: (*Without turning*) I can't find my braces anywhere.

TEMPLE crosses to a chest of drawers.

STEVE: Not much of a detective in real life, are you, my sweet! Try behind your back!

TEMPLE finds the braces and pulls them over his shoulders as he grins, ruefully.

TEMPLE: I'm still not used to being looked after, Steve.

STEVE: We've been married a year.

TEMPLE: A year today! And it seems like a week!

TEMPLE kisses STEVE.

STEVE: A lovely peaceful year, with no crime investigations, no adventures …

TEMPLE: And two new novels in the bag.

STEVE: Just you and me able to live our lives without being constantly badgered by Scotland Yard and Sir Graham Forbes!

TEMPLE: I like Forbes. He's a decent old stick.

STEVE: Paul, you're not sorry you promised to give up investigating crime when we got married?

TEMPLE: (*A shade too quickly*) Of course not, darling. It takes me all my time to find out what you're up to! Come on or we'll be late for our anniversary party! If we don't make a move, the Pompadour won't keep our table.

5

STEVE: You booked one all right?

TEMPLE: About the last. Everybody in town's going crazy
            over this singer they've got – Norma Rice.

As they go:

CUT TO: The Pompadour Club. Night.

The Pompadour is a top-class restaurant-club – a cross
between Ciro's and the Café de Paris before it was bombed.

At one side is the stage on which the dance band is seated.

There is a pass door at the side leading from the restaurant to
the corridor backstage off of which open the dressing rooms
used by the band and the cabaret artistes.

At the end is a magnificent staircase which gives access to the
swing doors leading to the foyer or entrance hall.

Then the staircase branches left to right, giving access to
balconies on each side of the room on which are tables for
guests who like to dine upstairs and look at the dancing floor
below.

*We open on NORMA RICE on the dance floor, singing a
number accompanied by the band.*

*She is lit by a single spot, consequently the rest of the room
and the tables can only be dimly seen, and it is difficult to
recognise faces.*

STEVE: This must be her first number. We haven't
            missed much.

TEMPLE: I hope not. She's very attractive.

TEMPLE smiles at STEVE.

He is only fooling.

NORMA RICE has now reached the refrain of her song.

*It is one of those numbers which enables her to sing to
individual tables in turn – a sort of "Is it you – or you – or
you?" type of song.*

Another spot picks out the different tables.

At one of them the spot picks out LEO BRENT and EDWARD LATHAM.

Eventually, the second spot hits the table next to TEMPLE and STEVE.

At it are seated SIR GRAHAM FORBES and a young man and a young woman.

TEMPLE: (*Whispering*) Look who's next to us!

STEVE: (*Looking*) It's old Forbes. Fancy being haunted by Scotland Yard on our anniversary!

TEMPLE: I suppose even Deputy Commissioners can have an evening off.

STEVE: If he tries to pull you in on a case again, I'll crown him with that bottle.

NORMA RICE finishes her number, and the lights come up. There is enthusiastic applause.

Then a buzz of conversation rises through the room and the band starts up a dance tune.

The young man and woman with FORBES join the other couples on the floor.

A WAITER brings a bottle of champagne to TEMPLE's table.

FORBES glances at their table, and then swings round in his chair.

FORBES: Temple!

TEMPLE: Nice to see you, Forbes. You remember Steve?

FORBES: As if I could forget her!

STEVE: I hope you mean that as a compliment, Sir Graham.

TEMPLE: Pull your chair round and join us in a drink.

FORBES pulls his chair round while TEMPLE pours out the champagne.

STEVE: I hope you're here on pleasure, not business.

FORBES: My niece and her young man wanted to see Norma Rice.

7

FORBES glances across to NORMA who is chatting to someone near the band.

FORBES: And as I've been working very hard just lately …

NORMA leaves her friends and vanishes through the pass-door.

TEMPLE: How are things at the Yard?

FORBES: Damnable, Temple.

TEMPLE: What's the trouble?

FORBES: It's these REX murders. There's three of 'em now. And we've got nowhere.

CUT TO: NORMA RICE's Dressing Room. Night.

MILLIE KENDALL, the dresser, is laying out NORMA RICE's costume for her next number.

The door opens and NORMA RICE enters.

NORMA: Anyone called to see me, Millie?

MILLIE: No, miss.

NORMA goes up to her dressing table and stands by it, drumming on the edge with her fingers.

She is clearly in a state of anxiety.

Then she makes up her mind.

She sits down at the dressing table, opens a drawer, takes out a pencil and paper and starts scribbling a note.

NORMA: Millie!

MILLIE: Yes, miss?

NORMA: Get hold of Charles and tell him to give this note to Sir Graham Forbes. Front row table, halfway down on the left.

We see what NORMA has written:

"SIR GRAHAM FORBES,

> *Will you come round and see me after my second number. I may be able to help you – about REX.*

>   *Norma Rice"*

NORMA finishes writing the note and gives it to MILLIE.

MILLIE: Now, miss?

MORMA: At once. It's very urgent.

MILLIE: (*Looking at NORMA's dress*) But you've got to change …

NORMA: I'll manage for myself. Off you go.

MILLIE goes out and NORMA goes to a screen behind which she changes.

CUT TO: Back Stage Corridor. Night.

MILLIE comes out of the dressing room and turns down the corridor.

A GIRL DRESSED IN GREY comes into view.

She passes MILLIE who gives her a casual glance and then walks on.

The GIRL IN GREY stops at the door of NORMA's dressing room, knocks, pauses a moment, and then goes in.

CUT TO: The Pompadour Club. Night.

The dance is still in progress.

SIR GRAHAM is still sitting with TEMPLE and STEVE continuing his account of the REX murders.

FORBES: And then last night a woman called Esther Van Ralston was found stabbed to death on the Canterbury-London Express, with REX scribbled on the blind. And not a clue of any description.

TEMPLE is enthralled.

He leans across the table towards FORBES.

TEMPLE: Nothing in her handbag to indicate –

STEVE: (*Interrupting TEMPLE*) Paul! Look who's coming along!

Threading their way through the tables towards TEMPLE and STEVE are LEO BRENT and EDWARD LATHAM.

9

LATHAM has a slight stutter on words beginning with 'R' and 'P'.

BRENT: Hello, there! You wouldn't look our way, so we had to come to you.

BRENT comes up to the table, LATHAM behind him.

TEMPLE: Leo Brent! It's grand to see you.

TEMPLE and BRENT shake hands.

BRENT: Glad to see you, Temple.

TEMPLE: I didn't know you were in England.

BRENT: Arrived last week. Steve! You look wonderful. How do you like double harness?

STEVE: Suits me!

TEMPLE: You don't know Sir Graham Forbes, do you?

TEMPLE turns to FORBES.

TEMPLE: This is Leo Brent. I saw a lot of him in the war, when I was attached to the Canadians.

FORBES: How d'you do?

BRENT: Glad to meet you. Now you've got to meet Ted Latham.

BRENT pulls LATHAM forward.

BRENT: This is Paul Temple and his wife.

LATHAM bows to STEVE who nods back.

LATHAM: Yours are the only detective novels I read, Mr Temple. I only hope the (*stutters*) police study them as closely as I do. They could learn a lot.

FORBES reacts slightly to this reference to the police. TEMPLE glances at him and grins.

TEMPLE: You'd better watch your step. This is Sir Graham Forbes – Deputy Commissioner at Scotland Yard.

FORBES: How d'you do?

LATHAM: The professional (*stutters*) – and the amateur. (*To BRENT*) This is an open championship meeting.

10

STEVE: My husband no longer competes, Mr
                Latham. Now he's married he sticks to his
                novels.

The MAITRE d'HOTEL enters.

HEAD WAITER: Excuse me, Sir Graham.

FORBES: What is it, Charles?

The MAITRE d'HOTEL hands FORBES a note.

HEAD WAITER: Miss Rice has asked me to see that you get
                this, sir.

FORBES: Will you excuse me?

FORBES turns back to his own table.

TEMPLE: What are you doing over here, Leo?

BRENT: Looking for a job – and a girlfriend.

STEVE: That lovely soldier stuff's out of date,
                Leo.

BRENT: Ted's fixing it for me! He's taking me
                round to see Norma Rice.

LATHAM: I've known Norma for years. I think she's
                just what Leo's looking for.

*All the time LATHAM's eyes keep switching over to FORBES'
table where FORBES has finished reading the note.*

FORBES: All right. Tell Miss Rice I'll come round.

HEAD WAITER: Very good, sir.

*The MAITRE d'HOTEL walks away whilst FORBES turns
back to TEMPLE's table.*

FORBES: You might like to have a look at this,
                Temple.

TEMPLE takes the note and starts to read it.

At this moment the dance band finishes a tune.

*It then plays a chord to indicate that the cabaret will now
continue.*

LATHAM: Norma's second number.

BRENT: We'd better get back to our table.

LATHAM: I'll join you in a moment. I just want to
                        make sure she's expecting us when it's
                        finished.

LATHAM moves off left.
Couples are leaving the floor.
*BRENT goes back to his table and FORBES' NIECE and her
FIANCE come back to FORBES' table.*
*We follow LATHAM as he crosses the floor to the pass-door.
He disappears and a moment later the general lighting dies
down.*
*Two spots, one from either side of the gallery come on in time
to pick up groups of chorus girls (3 or 6 from each side) who
enter and dance one refrain of the new number using the
grand staircase as their background and draping themselves
up either side of it to provide a setting for NORMA's entry.*
*A third spot then picks up NORMA at the head of the
staircase.*
*As she sings the number she advances slowly down the stairs
between the girls.*
*She continues the song for a few bars then suddenly falters
but recovers herself.*
TEMPLE is watching her intently.
*The number continues, then NORMA RICE suddenly clutches
at her throat and stops singing.*
FORBES begins to look puzzled.
He leans forward, frowning.
Anxiously he looks off towards the stairs.
*NORMA RICE is swaying in agony, and then suddenly
collapses.*
She pitches forward and crashes down the rest of the stairs.
She lies very still at the bottom.
The chorus girls rush to her side.
The band stops in mid-bar.

12

People get up from their tables to see what has happened. Women at the nearby tables scream.

FORBES and TEMPLE rush forward quickly, followed by waiters and other guests.

CUT TO: NORMA RICE's Dressing Room. Night.
NORMA RICE is lying on a couch behind the screen, and a DOCTOR is bending over her.

A group consisting of FORBES, TEMPLE and STEVE are looking in the mirror.

Behind them, MILLIE, the dresser, is hovering with tears streaming down her face, while the MAITRE d'HOTEL stands by her, obviously very upset at such a catastrophe in his Club.

On the mirror we see scrawled in lipstick on one corner REX.

FORBES: I – I can't believe it.

TEMPLE: It ties up with that note she sent you.

FORBES: If only the doctor can bring her round.

The DOCTOR appears from behind the screen.

They all crowd round him.

FORBES: Well?

The DOCTOR shakes his head.

FORBES: Dead?

DOCTOR: I'm afraid so.

MILLIE collapses into a chair, and STEVE goes over to comfort her.

The MAITRE d'HOTEL loses control.

He starts wringing his hands, and moaning.

HEAD WAITER: But it is terrible … terrible ... in the Pompadour … murder.

FORBES come up to him and shakes him roughly.

FORBES: Stop that, Charles. Go to the front entrance and wait for Inspector Crane.

13

I've telephoned for him. Directly he arrives bring him straight here.

HEAD WAITER: But … but …

FORBES: At once, please.

HEAD WAITER: But, Sir Graham.

The MAITRE d'HOTEL goes out of the door while FORBES joins TEMPLE and the DOCTOR.

TEMPLE: What killed her?

DOCTOR: I'm pretty sure she was poisoned.

FORBES: What kind of poison?

DOCTOR: Only an analysis can tell. There'll have to be an autopsy.

FORBES: But she was singing a number … out on the dance floor …

TEMPLE: Delayed reaction. That's possible with some poisons, isn't it?

DOCTOR: Certainly.

FORBES: But when can she have taken it?

TEMPLE: Perhaps Millie can help us.

TEMPLE crosses over to STEVE and MILLIE.

DOCTOR: There's nothing more I can do, Sir Graham.

FORBES: I'd like you to wait and see the police surgeon. He'll be coming along with Crane.

DOCTOR: Certainly, if you wish it.

STEVE listens and anxiously watches the concentrated expression on TEMPLE's face.

MILLIE: She never takes a bite nor a drink from teatime till after the Show.

TEMPLE: And she didn't this evening?

MILLIE: She did not.

TEMPLE: No one came to see her?

MILLIE: Only Mr Latham – but he's always popping in
            and out. Regular jack-in-the-box.
TEMPLE: Was Latham alone with Miss Rice?
MILLIE: Certainly not. I was in here all the time he was.
            He wasn't a minute. She was just running over
            her make-up, like she always did after dressing,
            and all he said was that he was bringing a friend
            round to see her after the show.
FORBES: So you were in here with her all the evening?
MILLIE: I was, except when I took that note to Charles.
            For you, sir.
TEMPLE: How long were you out of the room?
MILLIE: Not more'n a couple of minutes.
TEMPLE: You didn't see any strangers?
MILLIE: No, sir. Wait a minute! I did pass someone in the
            corridor.
FORBES: Who was it?
MILLIE: I don't know, sir.
TEMPLE: Man or woman?
MILLIE: Woman, sir. All dressed in grey she was, with
            grey 'andbag to match.
TEMPLE: Would you recognise her again?
MILLIE: No, sir. It's dingy in the corridor. I didn't rightly
            look at her face. But I'd know that 'andbag. Like
            a sausage it was.
FORBES: Did this woman come in here?
MILLIE: I don't know, sir. I never looked back to see.
*The door opens and INSPECTOR CRANE hurries in,
followed by a POLICE SURGEON, Finger-print Expert,
Photographer, etc.*
FORBES and TEMPLE turn towards the newcomers.
FORBES: Ah! There you are, Crane. (*Pointing behind the
            screen*) Doctor, will you have a word with the
            police surgeon?

15

The DOCTOR, Police Surgeon, Photographer, Finger-print Expert all move behind the screen followed by CRANE.

STEVE moves towards the dressing table out of their way. She takes a step forward, and her foot treads on something on the floor.

She bends down and picks it up and looks at it.

She is holding a lipstick.

On the case we see printed the one word – SULANG.

As STEVE looks at it a puzzled frown creases her forehead. Then she puts it down on the dressing table.

A flash goes off as the photographer exposes his first plate.

CRANE comes from behind the screen and joins FORBES, TEMPLE and STEVE near the dressing table.

FORBES: Crane, it's REX again.

CRANE: Good Lord!

FORBES: (*Pointing*) On the mirror.

TEMPLE: Or someone who wants us to think it's REX.

CRANE looks at TEMPLE as much as to say, "Who the hell are you".

His whole attitude is unfriendly.

FORBES: Do you know Mr Paul Temple, Crane?

CRANE: I know of him well enough, sir. How do?

TEMPLE smiles and nods to CRANE.

FORBES: (*To CRANE*) It was before your time when he used to work with us.

CRANE: I'd heard you'd found something better to do, Mr Temple.

STEVE: He got married, Inspector.

CRANE starts.

TEMPLE: This is my wife – Inspector Crane.

CRANE: Pleased to meet you. Well, I reckon we better get down to business.

STEVE: Come on, Paul.

TEMPLE: (*Puzzled*) Come on?

STEVE: We must go. We don't want to disturb the Inspector.

STEVE firmly takes TEMPLE's arm and moves towards the door.

TEMPLE: But Steve …

STEVE: We shall only be in the way.

FORBES: Mrs Temple, your husband can't go yet. I want his help.

STEVE: I'm sorry, Sir Graham. Tomorrow we are leaving for the country. Paul is starting a new book. You see, my husband is a novelist, not a detective. That's right, isn't it, Paul?

TEMPLE: (*Resignedly*) I'm afraid it is.

FORBES: But Temple –

TEMPLE: Sorry, Forbes. But a promise is a promise. I've retired from your racket.

TEMPLE and STEVE exit.

CUT TO: Back Stage Corridor. Night.

STEVE and TEMPLE come out from NORMA RICE's dressing room.

A UNIFORMED PC is on duty standing guard.

STEVE: Goodnight!

PC: Goodnight, madam – goodnight, sir.

TEMPLE: 'Night.

STEVE: I didn't like that man Crane much.

TEMPLE: No – hardly a friendly soul – still don't let that worry you, darling, (*wryly*) – as you pointed out we've finished with crime.

CUT TO: An Effect Montage

Superimpose over a library shot of printing presses running at speed newspaper headlines zooming up at different angles.

They include:-
NORMA RICE MURDERED BY REX
FOURTH REX MURDER IN A MONTH
SCOTLAND YARD BEWILDERED
WHAT ARE THE POLICE DOING ABOUT REX?
WHO IS THE MYSTERIOUS GIRL IN GREY?

CUT TO: The TEMPLE's Flat. Day.
The last paper in the montage is now seen to be in TEMPLE's hands as he sits in the lounge eagerly studying it.
He throws down the paper and bends down to pick up another.
All round him the floor is littered with other papers.
The clock on the mantelpiece strikes four.
TEMPLE looks up, puts down the paper with a sigh, and walks out of the sitting room into the hall.

CUT TO: The TEMPLE's Flat. Hall. Day.
TEMPLE enters from the lounge.
He pauses as he sees STEVE's suitcase and dressing case standing ready strapped up.
He sighs again, then goes into the bedroom.
From the doorway we see TEMPLE's suitcase lying open on the bed, half-packed.
TEMPLE flings a few more things into it, pauses again lost in thought, then pulls himself together, shuts the suitcase and carries it out into the hall.
The front doorbell rings.
TEMPLE puts the suitcase down by STEVE's cases, goes to the door, and opens it to reveal FORBES and CRANE.
TEMPLE: Come in, Forbes.
FORBES: Thank goodness we've caught you, Temple. I was afraid you might have started for the country.

FORBES and CRANE come in.

TEMPLE closes the door and points to the suitcases.

TEMPLE: You're only just in time. Steve's out doing some final shopping, but I'm expecting her any moment. Come in here.

TEMPLE leads the way into the lounge.

FORBES and CRANE follow.

FORBES: We've got to have a word with you.

CUT TO: A Top-Class Cosmetic Shop. London Street. Day.

STEVE comes out of the shop.

As she pauses on the pavement, the GIRL IN GREY hurries past.

We do not see her face but recognise her hat and her handbag which is long and round – in fact, like a sausage.

Steve, too, notices this.

With a gasp of astonishment, she hurries after the GIRL IN GREY who turns a corner.

CUT TO: A Crowded Pavement. London. Day.

STEVE is pushing her way through the throng of pedestrians and shoppers.

She turns into a side street but the GIRL IN GREY has vanished.

Disappointed, STEVE hails a taxi.

CUT TO: TEMPLE's Flat. The Lounge. Day.

FORBES and CRANE are sitting down, while TEMPLE is standing with his back to the fireplace, his pocket diary is in his hand.

TEMPLE: Now, let's see if I've got this straight. All four victims to date have been women?

CRANE: That's right.

TEMPLE: The first three murdered in trains?

FORBES: Correct.

TEMPLE looks at the diary he is holding.

We see that it says:

VICTIMS: MIRIAM JAMES

DODIE ALBRECHT and

ESTHER VAN RALSTON

TEMPLE: (*Reading*) "Their names were Miriam James, Dodie Albrecht and Esther Van Ralston." And in each case the letters REX were chalked on the blind.

CRANE: That's what strikes me as so corny. A modern murderer doesn't put his signature on the job.

TEMPLE: Unless he has a very good reason.

FORBES: What reason could he have?

TEMPLE: (*Ignoring the question*) Any trace of a motive common to all of 'em?

FORBES: Crane has some damn-fool theory of blackmail.

CRANE: In the first three cases they were all wealthy women. And I've ascertained that each has drawn large sums in cash a month or two before their death.

FORBES: But damn it, man, a blackmailer isn't such a fool as to bump off his victims. It's killing the goose that lays the golden eggs.

TEMPLE: Unless they'd refused to go on paying, and REX wanted to encourage other victims who were hesitating.

FORBES: Pour encourager les autres!

CRANE: You've got it! That'd explain him advertising himself as well!

FORBES: But what about Norma Rice? No trace of her being blackmailed.

TEMPLE:	REX killed her in self-protection. Her note to you makes that clear.
CRANE:	We've got a chance in her case. I'm combing London for the Girl in Grey.
TEMPLE:	You think she's REX?
CRANE:	I think she's the only person who could have bumped off Norma.
TEMPLE:	And there's no clue common to all these four cases?
CRANE:	Not to all four.
TEMPLE:	But something that occurs in more than one?
FORBES:	(*Slowly*) There was a name written in Miriam James' diary. The same name was scribbled on the back of a receipt bill which we found in Esther Van Ralston's handbag.
TEMPLE:	What was it?
FORBES:	Mrs Trevelyan.

From off-screen we hear the sound of a latch-key being inserted in a lock.

TEMPLE:	That'll be Steve.
FORBES:	(*Whispering hastily*) You will give us a hand?
TEMPLE:	(*Also whispering*) I'll do what I can, but don't let Steve know.

CUT TO: TEMPLE's Flat. The Hall. Day.
The front door opens, and STEVE comes in.
She shuts the front door and comes to the door of the lounge, where she pauses.
We hear the sound of a soda water syphon.

CUT TO: TEMPLE's Flat. The Lounge. Day.
TEMPLE is handing SIR GRAHAM and CRANE drinks.

FORBES: (*Trying to be casual*) You've not seen the show
             at the Palladium? You can't go out of Town till
             you've seen that. Your wife'd love it.

STEVE is now standing in the doorway.

She smiles at the transparent subterfuge and enters the room.

STEVE: Hello, Sir Graham. What a surprise!

FORBES and CRANE get up as STEVE enters.

FORBES: I was telling your husband it's a pity to rush out
             of Town so soon. I particularly want to take you
             both to the Palladium.

STEVE: There's nothing I'd love more. But I mustn't be
             selfish. Paul so much prefers the country.

FORBES' face falls, and STEVE bursts out laughing.

STEVE: You've been well and truly rumbled, Sir
             Graham. But there's nothing doing. The days
             when you could send for Paul Temple are past
             and gone.

FORBES: But dash it all, it was you who first made me
             send for him! That damned newspaper campaign
             you started when you were in Fleet Street drove
             me demented.

STEVE: I'm no longer a cub reporter. I'm a staid and
             unadventurous married woman who's going to
             make quite sure she's got a staid and
             unadventurous husband.

FORBES: But don't you realise –

STEVE: That you're in a tangle? But that's your funeral,
             and I don't want any funerals in our family.
             Come on, Paul. The car's at the door. Perhaps
             we can give you and the Inspector a lift, Sir
             Graham?

*TEMPLE smiles resignedly and goes to the door and opens
it.*

FORBES and CRANE look from wife to husband, then move out through the door, defeated.

CUT TO: A Country Main Road
TEMPLE's modern roadster is streaking along at a good pace.

CUT TO: Inside TEMPLE's Car.
STEVE is driving with her husband in the seat beside her. They are both lost in thought.
STEVE: (*Suddenly*) Sulang.
TEMPLE: What?
STEVE: Nothing.
There is a pause.
TEMPLE: Ever come across anyone called Mrs Trevelyan?
STEVE: I don't think so, why?
TEMPLE: I just wondered.
TEMPLE relapses into deep thought.
After a pause, Steve suddenly proclaims:
STEVE: That handbag was like a sausage.
TEMPLE: (*Absently*) I wouldn't worry. It's the Soya beans
               they put in them.
STEVE glances at TEMPLE, perplexed.

CUT TO: A Country Main Road
TEMPLE's car goes streaking along.
As it passes a side road a large black saloon car swings out and follows it.

CUT TO: Inside TEMPLE's Car.
TEMPLE and STEVE are both still lost in thought.
Then TEMPLE relaxes, sighs and concentrates on the countryside.

TEMPLE: Just coming up to Lenton Cutting. Good run, Steve.

STEVE: She's not pulling like she used to – I think it's time we got another car.

STEVE is looking into the driving mirror.

She frowns.

Somewhat distorted, we see the black Saloon about 50 yards behind them in the mirror.

The Saloon starts gaining on the Temples.

STEVE: In a hurry, isn't he?

TEMPLE: I'd let him pass.

STEVE signals the other car on.

It pulls out and starts to pass.

CUT TO: A Country Main Road

The black Saloon pulls out and comes alongside the Temples' car.

As it does so the driver, steering with his left hand, suddenly throws an object into the back of STEVE's car before accelerating and passing.

There is a crash of glass.

CUT TO: Inside TEMPLE's Car.

TEMPLE: What the devil's that? Pull up, Steve!

CUT TO: A Country Main Road.

The black Saloon races on and disappears.

TEMPLE's car pulls up at the side of the road.

CUT TO: Inside TEMPLE's Car.

TEMPLE turns and views with dismay the shattered window.

He looks down.

On the floor of the car a cylinder with brass terminals is lying – a bomb.

TEMPLE turns back.

TEMPLE: Quick, Steve – jump for it!

TEMPLE pushes STEVE out, leaning over to release her door – then exits from his own door.

CUT TO: A Country Main Road.

TEMPLE grabs STEVE's hand and races her across the road to the opposite side and flings themselves down on the ground.

TEMPLE's car goes up with a roar as the bomb explodes. It catches fire.

TEMPLE and STEVE pick themselves up.

Bits of debris and a wheel fall near them.

There is a flicker of flames.

TEMPLE: Darling, are you hurt?

STEVE: No, I don't think so ... only a bit shaken. What about you?

TEMPLE: No serious damage. Bit of a crack on the knee. By gosh we've been lucky!

The car is burning fiercely.

TEMPLE: What the insurance companies call a total loss – You said we wanted another car.

STEVE: But, Paul, what happened?

TEMPLE: That fellow in the black Saloon pitched a bomb of some kind into us. Did you notice his number?

STEVE: No.

TEMPLE: It was 639. But I'm not sure of the letters, except that there was a 'C' in them.

STEVE: But who should want to bump us off?

TEMPLE: I can only think of one person.

STEVE: REX?

25

TEMPLE: Your guess is as good as mine. Oh well, it's no
            good hanging about here. We'll have to hitch-
            hike to Bramley.

TEMPLE and STEVE turn away.

CUT TO: A Country Main Road.

*TEMPLE and STEVE walk along the road and stand by its
side.*

*TEMPLE looks back in the direction from which they have
come.*

TEMPLE: There's a car coming. You'd better do the
            thumbing, Steve. A pretty girl's always got more
            chance.

A frown has been gathering on STEVE's forehead.

She steps forward without replying.

The headlights of the car pick them up.

*As the car drives up, STEVE steps out into the road and
thumbs it.*

But it whizzes by ignoring them.

STEVE looks after the car, her frown getting deeper.

TEMPLE: Smile, Steve, or we won't have a chance!

*A lorry comes into sight proceeding in the opposite direction,
ie going back the way they have come.*

Suddenly STEVE steps forward and thumbs it.

There is a grinding of brakes, and the lorry pulls up.

TEMPLE hurries forward and catches STEVE by the arm.

TEMPLE: Hey, Steve, it's going the wrong way. Back to
            London.

STEVE: (*Blazing with anger*) If you think I'm going to
            allow a creature like REX to throw bombs into
            our car, you're daft!

*STEVE shakes her arm free and marches out into the road to
thumb down the lorry.*

26

TEMPLE stares after her, then a delighted grin spreads over his face.

TEMPLE: Atta, girl! That's the spirit!

TEMPLE hurries after STEVE.

The lorry stops and TEMPLE and STEVE speak to the driver who jerks his thumb round to the back.

They go round and climb onto the tailboard.

The lorry starts up and moves off.

CUT TO: Main Road. Night.

It is now nearly dark.

The lorry is driving away from where it picked TEMPLE and STEVE up.

A car comes up from behind, and in the light of its headlamps we see TEMPLE and STEVE sitting on the tailboard.

STEVE: You see, Sulang is one of the latest cosmetics. It's made in Egypt. Unobtainable in this country.

TEMPLE: You're certain?

STEVE: I tried a dozen shops and they all told me the same thing.

TEMPLE: And it was outside a cosmetic shop you saw the Girl in Grey?

STEVE: Yes. D'you think she could be REX, Paul?

TEMPLE: I haven't started to think yet. The first thing to do is try and trace that car. And that's a job for my old friend, Spider Williams.

STEVE: What about Sir Graham?

TEMPLE: When we've got something to go on we'll offer him our joint services.

STEVE: On one condition.

TEMPLE: What's that?

STEVE: That first thing tomorrow I go out and try and get someone to replace Rikki. I refuse to tackle the housekeeping and a criminal investigation at the same time.

TEMPLE: O.K. Whatever you say. Which reminds me, is there anything in the flat for breakfast?

STEVE: There should be some bacon about.

The headlights of an over-taking car illuminate the interior of the lorry and we see that hanging all around TEMPLE and STEVE are sides of bacon.

TEMPLE: You're telling me.

CUT TO: TEMPLE's Flat. Kitchen. Day.

STEVE is frying three small rashers of bacon in a pan.

STEVE: (*Calling*) How does your Mr Williams like his bacon? Crisp or underdone?

CUT TO: TEMPLE's Flat. The Bedroom. Day.

TEMPLE is in his shirt-sleeves, brushing his hair in front of the mirror.

TEMPLE: (*Calling back*) I haven't a clue. I've never entertained him to breakfast.

CUT TO: TEMPLE's Flat. Kitchen. Day.

STEVE: Then he'll have to take it as it comes. It's our ration anyway.

STEVE dishes up the bacon, puts the dish on three plates and carries it out into the hall.

CUT TO: TEMPLE's Flat. The Hall. Day.

STEVE enters from the kitchen.

She is just going into the living room when the flat doorbell rings.

STEVE, still carrying the bacon, goes to the door and opens it, then starts back with a gasp of alarm, dropping the dish and plates on to the floor.

In the doorway is the ogre-like figure of a man in dirty, dishevelled clothes and with a sinister leer on his ugly and unshaven face.

It is SPIDER WILLIAMS.

SPIDER: (*Very sinister*) Mr Temple in?

STEVE: Go away.

STEVE tries to shut the door, but SPIDER puts his foot against it and advances.

SPIDER: I gotta see Mr Temple.

STEVE: (*Retreating*) He's not in. Go away.

SPIDER advances into the hall.

Just as STEVE is about to scream, TEMPLE comes out of the bedroom into the hall.

TEMPLE: Hello, Spider, just in time for breakfast.

TEMPLE sees the broken plates and mangled bacon on the floor.

TEMPLE: No, you're not. You're just too late.

STEVE: But, Paul, you don't mean –

TEMPLE: Of course I do. This is my old pal Spider Williams, who knows more about the stolen car racket than any living soul. Spider, meet my wife.

SPIDER: It's a pleasure.

SPIDER reaches out a bony hand and nearly shakes STEVE's hand off.

STEVE: If I don't succeed in getting a servant, Paul, I shall leave you.

CUT TO: TEMPLE's Flat. The Lounge. Day.

TEMPLE, STEVE and SPIDER are sitting round the table, having finished breakfast.

SPIDER: So I didn't waste no time after you telephoned last night, but I 'ad to get 'old of Ernie an' 'e

29

wasn't sober enough to get crackin' till six o'clock this morning.

TEMPLE: Well, I'll bet Ernie had a nasty hangover.

SPIDER: Somethin' cruel. And as usual 'e was most blarstpheemous.

TEMPLE grins at STEVE.

TEMPLE: But did he deliver the goods?

SPIDER: In a manner of speaking. The only job last evening 'e knew of was a black Riley Saloon.

STEVE: (*Eagerly*) That's right.

SPIDER: D.R.C. 639.

TEMPLE: (*Excited*) That fits.

SPIDER: But it weren't stolen. It was only borrowed.

TEMPLE: Borrowed?

SPIDER: Yes. By the chauffeur wot drives it.

TEMPLE: Where did he borrow it from?

SPIDER: Lacey's Garage, Great Portland Mews. An' it's back there this minute, all tiddley-poo.

STEVE: Tiddley-poo?

SPIDER: As good as noo.

TEMPLE: But who does it belong to?

SPIDER: I got that for you.

SPIDER pulls a dirty piece of paper out of his pocket, and hands it to TEMPLE, who gazes at it.

STEVE jumps up and looks at the paper over TEMPLE's shoulder.

TEMPLE: (*Reading*) Dr Kohima, 497 Wimpole Street!

CUT TO: Wimpole Street. Day.

There is general activity in the street.

CUT TO: KOHIMA's House. Day.

Two middle-aged Society women are coming down the steps – the door just closing behind them.

30

It is obvious from their clothes that they are well-to-do –
typical patients, in fact, of a fashionable psychoanalyst.
1st LADY: My dear Mary, he's too marvellous.
We see the brass-plate on the front door bearing the words:
DR CHARLES KOHIMA.

CUT TO: The Waiting Room. Wimpole Street. Day.
It is a typical Specialist's Waiting Room, with a large dining
table in the centre, covered with periodicals, and chairs
round the walls, two of which are occupied by another couple
of typical Society women.
Seated at the table is TEMPLE, the only man in the room.
He is trying to cover his embarrassment by pretending to look
at a periodical.
He finds it difficult to concentrate and keeps looking up, only
to drop his eyes again quickly before the barrage of female
stares.
The door of the waiting room opens and the RECEPTIONIST
ushers in EDWARD LATHAM.
She does not speak, but we have time to notice that she is
dressed in grey – although we do not yet know who she is.
She beckons the two women who rise and follow her out.
TEMPLE greets LATHAM.
TEMPLE: Hello, Latham!
LATHAM looks doubtful for a moment, then his face clears.
LATHAM: Why, it's Paul Temple! I never imagined you as
           a patient of Dr Kohima.
LATHAM sits on the edge of the table by TEMPLE.
TEMPLE: I'm not a patient – I want some local colour for
           my new book. What's your trouble?
LATHAM: Nerves, Mr Temple. I've always been very
           highly strung since I was a child.
TEMPLE: And you find the doctor can help you?

31

LATHAM:	Immeasurably. He's quite brilliant, you know. I first heard of him when I was in Cairo some years ago. He was the leading Egyptian psychoanalyst. When I've experienced a sudden nerve strain like that ghastly business of poor darling Norma, I rush straight to him.
TEMPLE:	I see.
LATHAM:	I do hope Scotland Yard will find the blackguard who murdered her.
TEMPLE:	So does Sir Graham.
LATHAM:	(*Eagerly*) Have they made any progress?

The door opens and the RECEPTIONIST enters.

RECEPTIONIST:	Mr Temple, please.

TEMPLE rises.

TEMPLE:	I'm afraid I wouldn't know. Well, so long, Latham. We'll meet again soon, I hope.
LATHAM:	You'll always find me at the Pompadour. I really believe it's the best food in London.

TEMPLE goes out of the door followed by the RECEPTIONIST.

CUT TO:	The Entrance Hall. Wimpole Street. Day.
RECEPTIONIST:	As you see, the doctor's very busy, Mr Temple. Will you be very long with him?
TEMPLE:	I don't think so. I'm not going to discuss my symptoms.
RECEPTIONIST:	(*Smiling*) So I gathered from our telephone conversation.
TEMPLE:	That's right. It was you I spoke to?
RECEPTIONIST:	Yes, I'm his secretary. My name's Mrs Trevelyan.

TEMPLE quickly controls his instinctive reaction, which apparently escapes MRS TREVELYAN as she moves down the hall past a table in a recess on which stands a telephone.

TREVELYAN: This way, please.

Still staring at her, TEMPLE follows.

He glances at the telephone.

MRS TREVELYAN pauses outside another door.

She puts her hand to open it, then turns back to TEMPLE.

TREVELYAN: You are the Mr Temple, aren't you?

TEMPLE: I'm Paul Temple, if that's what you mean.

TREVELYAN: You work with Scotland Yard, don't you?

TEMPLE: Not now. I'm just a hard-working writer.

MRS TREVELYAN opens the door and stands aside to let TEMPLE enter.

As TEMPLE goes into the room, MRS TREVELYAN is biting her lip as if in indecision.

CUT TO: KOHIMA's Consulting Room. Day.

KOHIMA is sitting in a swivel chair in front of a large desk on which stand several imposing medical books and also the drawer of a small card index box containing his case cards.

There is no telephone in the room.

As TEMPLE enters, he swings the chair round.

KOHIMA: Good morning, Mr Temple. Please sit down.

KOHIMA indicates a chair by the end of the desk.

TEMPLE: Thank you.

TEMPLE sits down and KOHIMA pushes a large box of cigarettes towards him.

KOHIMA: Cigarette?

TEMPLE: Thank you.

KOHIMA lights it for him.

TEMPLE takes the opportunity of glancing rapidly over the contents of the desk.

33

KOHIMA:	Now, Mr Temple, what can I do for you?
TEMPLE:	Frankly, answer a few questions.
KOHIMA:	That will be a change for me. It's usually I who ask the questions. I understand what you want is local colour.
TEMPLE:	Exactly. You own a black Riley Saloon, I believe?
KOHIMA:	(*Surprised*) I do. But –
TEMPLE:	Number DRC 639.
KOHIMA:	That's right.
TEMPLE:	Where d'you garage it?
KOHIMA:	Lacey's Garage, Great Portland Mews.
TEMPLE:	When did you last use it?
KOHIMA:	The day before yesterday.
TEMPLE:	You didn't take it out of the garage yesterday at all?
KOHIMA:	Definitely not.
TEMPLE:	Would you mind ringing up the garage and asking them who did take the car out?
KOHIMA:	I'm afraid I'm getting a little out of my depth, Mr Temple.
TEMPLE:	I'm very interested in your car, Dr Kohima.
KOHIMA:	Apparently. But may I ask why?
TEMPLE:	Because at about six o'clock last night, the driver of your car pitched a bomb into mine.
KOHIMA:	(*Completely astonished*) What?
TEMPLE:	It was sheer luck that both I and my wife escaped.
KOHIMA:	But it's impossible! I tell you, I didn't take it out yesterday at all.
TEMPLE:	But someone else may have. That's why I'm asking you to telephone.
KOHIMA:	I don't have a telephone in here. It disturbs me with my patients.

34

TEMPLE: But there's one in the hall.

KOHIMA rises from his chair.

KOHIMA: Perhaps you would like to come with me and speak to the garage yourself?

TEMPLE: *(Sitting back in his chair)* I'm quite content to leave it to you, Doctor.

KOHIMA stares at TEMPLE for a moment, then goes out into the hall, shutting the door behind him.

TEMPLE leans back lazily in his chair, one hand in his pocket, but directly he hears the sound of the door closing, he is galvanized into action.

He pulls his hand out of his pocket and puts his pocket diary on the desk.

Then he pulls the drawer of the card index towards him.

We see that TEMPLE's diary is open at the page which he was looking at in his flat when talking to FORBES and CRANE.

We can read: VICTIMS: MIRIAM JAMES, DODIE ALBRECHT, ESTHER VAN RALSTON.

We see Temple's fingers quickly flicking over the case cards. He pulls one up about half-an-inch. We read: ALBRECHT, DODIE.

He pushes it back in, and flicks on till he pulls up another card – JAMES, MIRIAM, and so finally to VAN RALSTON, ESTHER.

CUT TO: KOHIMA's Hall. Day.

KOHIMA is on the phone.

KOHIMA: I see. Thank you.

KOHIMA hangs up and moves towards his consulting room door.

CUT TO: KOHIMA's Consulting Room. Day.

TEMPLE is at the desk.

He puts his diary away and then with a quick glance round opens the top-right-hand drawer of the desk.
There is an automatic lying in it.
TEMPLE's hand quickly closes the drawer but does not quite shut it.
KOHIMA hurries back into the room looking very perturbed. He rejoins TEMPLE.

KOHIMA: Mr Temple, I owe you an apology.

TEMPLE: In other words, the garage confirms that your car was taken out yesterday?

KOHIMA: They say my chauffeur fetched the car about 5pm and brought it back about 7.30pm. But – it doesn't make sense!

TEMPLE: Why not?

KOHIMA: (*Slowly*) Because, Mr Temple, my chauffeur happens to be on holiday in Ireland.

There is a pause whilst TEMPLE digests this information. Then he rises.

TEMPLE: Well, Dr Kohima, I mustn't take up any more of your time. Mrs Trevelyan told me you were very busy.

KOHIMA: What are you going to do?

TEMPLE: What more can I do? Except to thank you for being so frank.

KOHIMA and TEMPLE walk to the door.

KOHIMA: Are you going to report it to the police?

TEMPLE: I'm afraid they won't have much time for murder attempts that have failed. You see they are concentrating on those that have succeeded.

TEMPLE turns and walks out of the room.

CUT TO: The Entrance Hall. Wimpole Street. Day.
TEMPLE walks towards the front door.

Just as he is opposite the waiting room door, which is ajar, we hear the off-screen MRS TREVELYAN's voice.

MRS TREVELYAN's VOICE: Mr Temple!

TEMPLE turns.

MRS TREVELYAN is hurrying down the stairs towards TEMPLE, an anxious worried expression on her face.

TREVELYAN: Mr Temple, I want to have a talk with you … a private talk. I'm … I'm very worried.

TEMPLE: What about?

TREVELYAN: I can't tell you … here. I need your advice … your help. Will you come and see me at my house … 49 Marshall House Terrace … tonight at 6.30 … it's terribly urgent …

From off-screen we hear a buzzer.

TREVELYAN: That's the doctor … I must go … please, oh please, don't fail me.

MRS TREVELYAN hurries into the consulting room.

TEMPLE turns and tries to open the front door, which however is securely locked.

From off-screen we hear KOHIMA's voice.

KOHIMA's VOICE: It's your own fault you're locked in, Mr Temple.

TEMPLE turns and sees KOHIMA who is smiling as he stands in the doorway of his consulting room.

KOHIMA: It's a little gadget of mine in case any of my patients are troublesome. If the top right-hand drawer of my desk is opened, it automatically locks the front door. (*He turns back to the room*) Mrs Trevelyan! Please!

There is a click and when TEMPLE again tries the door it opens.

TEMPLE: Thank you, Doctor. I'll know next time.

KOHIMA: You won't forget?

37

TEMPLE: No, I shan't forget.

CUT TO: TEMPLE's Flat. The Hall. Day.
The front door is opened from the outside and TEMPLE hurries in putting away his latchkey.
He stands in the middle of the hall taking off his hat and coat.
TEMPLE: Steve! Where are you?
STEVE's VOICE: (*From the bedroom*) I'm changing.
Simultaneously, out of the kitchen door, which is behind TEMPLE, RIKKI has emerged and has taken PAUL's hat from his hand as he struggles out of his coat.
RIKKI then takes the coat, but TEMPLE is too absorbed to notice.
TEMPLE: I've got a lot to tell you. I –
TEMPLE suddenly realises that someone must have taken his hat and coat.
He swings round.
TEMPLE: Rikki! What the devil are you doing here?
RIKKI: You will rejoice to hear that I have returned to the fold, Mr Temple.
STEVE comes out of the bedroom and stands watching them, thoroughly amused.
TEMPLE: (*Turning to STEVE*) You don't mean you've –?
STEVE: Rikki was the only one available, Paul.
RIKKI: Since leaving you, Mr Temple, I have attended to the wants of a single gentleman, and then of an unhappily married couple. But then I was unable to settle in either situation because all my thoughts have remained centred on you and your welfare. My dearest wish is to ensure your comfort and –
TEMPLE: (*Interrupting RIKKI*) Listen, Rikki. If I've got to put up with you again, here are three 'don'ts' for you. First, don't talk so much.

38

RIKKI: No, Mr Temple. I shall merely address to you the necessary words for performing my daily tasks.

TEMPLE: (*Swallowing*) Second, don't serve up any more Burmese dishes.

RIKKI: But my mother in Rangoon has sent me a recipe –

TEMPLE: (*Interrupting savagely*) And finally, and most important – don't fuss over me!

RIKKI: No, Mr Temple.

TEMPLE turns away, when RIKKI suddenly makes a dash at him and clutches him by the arm.

TEMPLE: What the devil –

RIKKI picks something off TEMPLE's collar and holds it up triumphantly.

RIKKI: A speck of fluff – on your jacket collar.

Thoroughly exasperated, TEMPLE marches off into the lounge, followed by the convulsed STEVE.

They shut the door.

RIKKI looks after them smiling benignly.

He then looks at the hat, shakes his head sadly, picks up a clothes brush from the hall table, and stands brushing it energetically.

CUT TO: TEMPLE's Flat. The Lounge. Day.

STEVE is sitting on the arm of TEMPLE's chair.

STEVE: Then Mrs Trevelyan must be the girl in grey?

TEMPLE: She was dressed in grey all right.

STEVE: Did you see her handbag?

TEMPLE: No.

STEVE: What age is she? What does she look like?

TEMPLE: About thirty. But she's a very attractive woman.

STEVE: And she's asked you to go round and see her in Marshall House Terrace tonight!

TEMPLE: That's right. 6.30.
STEVE: D'you think it's a trap?
TEMPLE: She seemed genuinely worried. Anyhow, I must
            go.
STEVE: You mean, we must go.
TEMPLE: Now, listen to me, Steve –
STEVE: (*Interrupting TEMPLE*) You listen to me, my
            sweet! If you think I'm going to let you call on
            'very attractive women' in their homes after
            office hours all on your little lonesome, you
            must be crackers.
STEVE walks to the door.
TEMPLE: Where are you going?
STEVE: To change my clothes.
TEMPLE: But you were changing when I came in.
STEVE: I'm putting on my best, my love.
STEVE leaves.

CUT TO: A Street Nameplate reading MARSHALL
            HOUSE TERRACE.

CUT TO: Marshall House Terrace. Night.
It is an ordinary residential street in Bayswater or Kensington.
*TEMPLE and STEVE walk down the street, then turn into one
of the houses.*

CUT TO: The Front Door and Hall of 49 Marshall House
            Terrace.
TEMPLE rings the bell.
*STEVE takes out her compact and checks her face in the
mirror.*
STEVE: D'you like my hat?
TEMPLE: Very much.
STEVE: Couldn't you be a little more enthusiastic?

TEMPLE: (*Grinning and taking STEVE's arm*) I believe you've got the wind up.

STEVE: Why should I have? There's no danger.

TEMPLE: I meant about Mrs Trevelyan's attraction.

STEVE: Nonsense. In any case, she's got shocking manners, not to answer the bell.

TEMPLE rings again.

There is a pause.

Suddenly STEVE shudders.

STEVE: Lonely sort of road, isn't it?

TEMPLE: Just what I was thinking.

There is a pause.

STEVE: Paul, I don't believe there's anyone in.

TEMPLE takes hold of the knocker, but before he can use it, the door swings gently open.

STEVE gives a startled exclamation.

STEVE: Oh!

TEMPLE: It wasn't shut!

TEMPLE pushes the door open, and they look down an ordinary entrance hall, from which stairs lead up into the darkness.

Halfway along the hall is an open door, from which light penetrates into the dark hall.

TEMPLE: Perhaps the bell's out of order. Let's go in.

TEMPLE and STEVE enter.

CUT TO: The Living Room. Marshall House Terrace. Night.

The room is comfortable and pleasantly furnished.

It is lit by two standard lamps which are both on.

The gas fire is burning in the grate.

Against one wall is a flat-topped writing desk.

On the mantelpiece is an ormolu clock with the hands at 6.30.

Its ticking echoes through the room.

41

TEMPLE and STEVE appear in the doorway.
They look into the room and then come in.

TEMPLE: Perhaps she's upstairs. We'll wait.

TEMPLE pushes the door half to.
He and STEVE wander about the room, summing it up.

STEVE: What a row that clock makes!

TEMPLE: At any rate, we're punctual. 6.30 to the dot.
           Look!

TEMPLE points to a suitcase which is standing by the wall
close to the fireplace.

TEMPLE: She must be in the house. If she'd done a flit,
           that wouldn't be here.

TEMPLE wanders off towards the desk.
STEVE looks round and again gives a little shiver.
She is clearly apprehensive.

TEMPLE: Come and look at this.

STEVE joins TEMPLE who has picked up a piece of paper
from the desk.
It reads: MARY ANDERSON
LADY HACKWILL
AGATHA LADYCROSS
MAY HADINGHAM
Whenever it occurs the letter 'a' is slightly out of alignment.
Underneath the typewritten words is a note in ink:
Sent B.T.

TEMPLE: Interesting!

STEVE: It doesn't mean much to me.

TEMPLE: All the same, I'll take it.

TEMPLE folds the paper and puts it in his pocket.
STEVE strolls off to take another look round the room.
TEMPLE continues to look over the desk.
Then he leans over the blotting pad.

The top sheet of blotting paper is clean, except for a few marks in the centre which look as if they might be the result of an envelope being blotted.

STEVE has wandered over to the mantelpiece.

Suddenly she bends forward and stares intently at the clock. The hands are still at 6.30.

She looks at her watch which shows nearly 6.40.

She leans forward and gets her ear as close as possible to the clock.

TEMPLE is still at the desk.

He has removed the top sheet of blotting paper and is just putting it in his pocket when STEVE calls out.

STEVE: Paul!

TEMPLE joins STEVE by the fireplace.

STEVE: Paul! The hands of the clock haven't moved.

TEMPLE: No, they haven't! Funny! It's ticking away all right.

STEVE: No, it isn't. The ticking isn't coming from the clock.

TEMPLE: Where's it coming from, then?

STEVE: (*Pointing to the suitcase*) From there.

TEMPLE drops to his knees by the suitcase and listens. STEVE does the same.

TEMPLE: (*Urgently*) Steve, get the hell out of here!

STEVE: What d'you mean?

TEMPLE: Get out into the road, quick!

STEVE: Not unless you do.

TEMPLE: Then get behind that sofa – only move!

STEVE draws back and TEMPLE gingerly opens the suitcase.

We see that inside it is a black canister, which contains explosive materials and which is connected by wires to a kind of time-fuse apparatus from which the ticking emerges louder than ever.

43

Quickly, but very delicately, TEMPLE disconnects the wires joining the time fuse apparatus to the bomb.

TEMPLE: By gosh, it's pretty lucky I was in the Sappers in the War.

STEVE comes back to TEMPLE.

STEVE: What is this, Paul?

TEMPLE: A bomb, my love. Connected to a clock fuse. If that had stopped ticking –

The ticking stops.

STEVE: (*Clutching TEMPLE's arm*) It's stopped now.

TEMPLE: If it had stopped three seconds ago, we'd have been blown sky-high.

TEMPLE wipes his forehead.

STEVE sinks back on her haunches.

STEVE: Paul … I think I'm going to be sick.

CUT TO: SIR GRAHAM FORBES' Office. Scotland Yard. Night.

FORBES is sitting at his desk.

On the desk stands the suitcase containing the bomb and clock-fuse.

Round the desk are sitting TEMPLE, STEVE and INSPECTOR CRANE.

FORBES: Frankly, I'm just in a muddle. What about you, Crane?

CRANE: It all seems so disjointed. Nothing fits together.

TEMPLE: Supposing we just tot up what we know?

FORBES: All right. Go ahead.

TEMPLE: Let's start with Norma Rice. I presume you are satisfied she was murdered?

FORBES: Looks like it. She died from the effects of some obscure poison apparently contained in her lipstick.

STEVE: … which was made in Egypt!

CRANE: She'd hardly choose that way if she wanted to commit suicide.

TEMPLE: Steve and I – and you, Forbes – were there at the time. The next day REX tries to bump off Steve and myself, using Dr Kohima's car. We traced it, and I find that the first victims of REX were all patients of Dr Kohima's.

STEVE: And we also find that the Doctor's secretary is Mrs Trevelyan, whose name is connected with two of the murders.

TEMPLE: And she's dressed in grey, is obviously worried and anxious and makes a date for me to call on her –

STEVE: – and is so attractive that we both go – and nearly get blown to bits by a time bomb.

FORBES looks from one to the other.

FORBES: Well, I must say that makes it as clear as mud! And where do we go from here?

CRANE: There's only one tenable theory. REX isn't one person, he's two. Kohima and Mrs Trevelyan, alias the Girl in Grey.

FORBES: By Jove, Crane, I believe you've hit it.

CRANE: It fits all the known facts. Kohima's an Egyptian.

FORBES: We'd better pick 'em both up at once.

TEMPLE: One minute, Forbes. I think the Inspector's forgotten the important clues we picked up in Marshall House Terrace.

CRANE: What were they?

TEMPLE: This.

TEMPLE picks up the typewritten list of names.

CRANE: Just four names. No help at all.

TEMPLE: But we may trace who typed it. Look at the 'a' – out of alignment.

45

CRANE grunts sarcastically.

TEMPLE: Then, there's the – blotting paper –

TEMPLE picks the blotting paper off the desk too.

TEMPLE: – which, as you've seen, when held to a mirror, shows Mrs Trevelyan addressed a letter to Miss Judy Grant, The Falcon Hotel, Canterbury.

CRANE: Well, where does that get you?

TEMPLE gets up and helps STEVE up.

TEMPLE: After I've had a night's sleep, it's going to get me to Canterbury. If you don't mind, Forbes, I think we'll get along. It's been rather a strenuous twenty-four hours for Steve.

STEVE: I'm fine.

FORBES also rises.

FORBES: Then you don't want us to pick up Mrs Trevelyan and Kohima?

TEMPLE: Not yet. If I change my mind, I'll ring you tomorrow morning.

FORBES: Very well, I'll see you out.

TEMPLE: Don't bother. I remember my way – from the old days!

TEMPLE and STEVE go out of the room, and CRANE shuts the door behind them.

Then he comes up to the desk.

CRANE: You're going to let him have his head?

FORBES: It's always paid in the past.

CRANE: You're sure he's – all right?

FORBES: Of course I am. Aren't you?

CRANE: Never did trust those amateurs!

CUT TO: TEMPLE's Flat. The Lounge. Day.

TEMPLE is dialling a number on the telephone.

STEVE is sitting on the edge of a chair.

TEMPLE: I hope I can catch old Spider.

STEVE: And while he's busy identifying the mysterious chauffeur, what do we do?

TEMPLE: Check up Kohima's typewriter and see if that list of names we found in Mrs Trevelyan's house was typed on it.

STEVE: And then – Canterbury and Judy Grant!

TEMPLE: (*Into the telephone*) Hello … That you, Spider? … It's Paul Temple … Any news?

STEVE gets up and strolls over to the window.

TEMPLE: (*On phone*) Listen, Spider … It wasn't the chauffeur who took that car. He was in Ireland.

STEVE turns and gazes out of the window as she listens to what PAUL is saying.

TEMPLE: … It was someone dressed up to look like him …

Suddenly, something on the pavement below catches STEVE's eye.

She leans forward and looks down.

We see what STEVE sees.

A taxi draws up.

The GIRL In GREY, complete with handbag, gets out and pays the taxi driver.

STEVE: (*Excitedly*) Paul!

TEMPLE is still on the phone.

TEMPLE: … Spider, you've got to find out who it really was … Yes, vitally urgent …

STEVE: Paul! Quick!

TEMPLE: Ring me the moment you've any news.

TEMPLE rings off and gets up.

STEVE is leaning half out of the window.

STEVE: Look, Paul!

TEMPLE joins STEVE and looks down.

The GIRL IN GREY walks across the pavement and into the block of flats.

We cannot see her face.

TEMPLE: The Girl in Grey!

STEVE: But – why's she coming here?

TEMPLE: If Crane's theory is right, to make sure
                we're bumped off this time.

The doorbell rings.

STEVE clutches TEMPLE's arm.

STEVE: Let Rikki answer it.

TEMPLE: Of course – and I hope she shoots straight.

TEMPLE goes to the door of the lounge.

CUT TO: TEMPLE's Flat. The Hall. Day.

RIKKI comes out of the kitchen, struggling into his housecoat.
He sees TEMPLE in the doorway of the lounge.

RIKKI: Do not disturb yourself, Mr Temple. To
                answer the front door is one of my
                pleasures.

RIKKI hurries towards the front door.
TEMPLE steps back so he is out of sight of the front door.

CUT TO: TEMPLE's Flat. The Lounge. Day.

TEMPLE and STEVE are standing just inside the lounge and
are listening intently to what is happening in the hall.

WOMAN's VOICE: Is Mr Temple in?

An expression of astonishment comes over TEMPLE's face.
He steps forward into the hall, followed by STEVE.

CUT TO: TEMPLE's Flat. The Hall. Day.

Standing in the doorway, dressed in black, is MRS
TREVELYAN.

TEMPLE: Good morning.

TREVELYAN: Mr Temple, I must apologise –

TEMPLE: Please don't. I'm delighted to see you. This
                is my wife; Steve, this is Mrs Trevelyan.

STEVE: (*Stifling a gasp*) How – how d'you do?

TEMPLE: Come in here, Mrs Trevelyan.

TEMPLE stands aside while STEVE and MRS TREVELYAN go into the lounge.

RIKKI sidles up to TEMPLE and flicks some dust off his back. TEMPLE swings round, startled.

RIKKI: Dust on your jacket, Mr Temple.

TEMPLE: (*Angrily*) I like dust on my jacket.

TEMPLE goes into the lounge, shutting the door.

RIKKI smiles after him indulgently.

Then he turns and starts to whistle, remembers himself, and goes into the kitchen.

CUT TO: TEMPLE's Flat. The Lounge. Day.

MRS TREVELYAN and STEVE are sitting while TEMPLE has taken up his usual position with his back to the mantelpiece.

TREVELYAN: I've come to apologise about last night, Mr Temple.

TEMPLE: Yes?

TREVELYAN: I don't know whether you did come to Marshall House Terrace?

TEMPLE: I did. And my wife came with me.

TREVELYAN: You must have thought me terribly rude.

STEVE: (*Involuntarily*) Rude!

TREVELYAN: Actually, I was the victim of a hoax.

TEMPLE: Really?

TREVELYAN: Just before 6.30 the telephone rang, and a man's voice asked me to come immediately to the hotel at the top of the road. It was urgent. Vitally urgent. A – very dear friend of mine was in danger.

TEMPLE: So you went?

TREVELYAN:	I rushed out immediately. And when I got there, there was no sign of him – of my friend. I made enquiries. The hotel knew nothing about it. By the time I got back you must have gone.
TEMPLE:	What bad luck! But perhaps you'll tell me now, what you wanted to see me about?
TREVELYAN:	I want you to help me with the police.
TEMPLE:	Why should you need help with the police?
TREVELYAN:	I'm terrified that they will try and implicate me in these REX murders.
STEVE:	(*Gasping*) REX!
TEMPLE:	Why on earth should they, Mrs Trevelyan?
TREVELYAN:	I've been reading in the papers about this Girl in Grey. I somehow feel she's suspected.
TEMPLE:	D'you know who she is?
TREVELYAN:	I believe they think I'm the Girl in Grey.
TEMPLE:	Why should they?
TREVELYAN:	Because – until today – I've always worn grey. Also, I seem to answer exactly to the description published in the paper. And I believe I'm being followed.
TEMPLE:	Followed?
TREVELYAN:	Yes. I'm – I'm sure of it. And, Mr Temple, I mustn't get tangled up with the police. It'll ruin my job … and Dr Kohima. It'll be fatal for his practice. And I thought perhaps you could explain … I know they'll listen to you … I've typed a list of all my movements, these last few days …

MRS TREVELYAN hurriedly pulls some papers out of her handbag.

50

TREVELYAN: ... This'll show I couldn't have had anything to do with it ...

MRS TREVELYAN holds out the papers.

TREVELYAN: ... Please, Mr Temple ...

TEMPLE takes the papers, but before he can look at them the telephone rings.

He picks up the receiver.

TEMPLE: (*On the phone*) Hello ... Paul Temple speaking ...

For the duration of this conversation, we intercut between TEMPLE in the lounge and SIR GRAHAM FORBES in his office.

CRANE is standing beside SIR GRAHAM.

FORBES: Listen, Temple. I'm not at all happy about what we arranged. As Crane says, it's madness not to pick up the Doctor and the Trevelyan woman ...

CRANE nods his head.

TEMPLE: I wouldn't do that.

FORBES: Crane's certain she's phoney. He's laid on to have her tailed ...

TEMPLE: The devil he has! Then tell him to lay it off as quickly as possible.

FORBES: But, Temple, I agree with him. We've got to get a move on. I've had the Home Secretary on the telephone half the morning ... and he's as irritable as blazes ...

TEMPLE: You don't need to bother about him. Leave it to me, there's a good girl!

FORBES: What d'you mean, there's a good girl ... Dash it, Temple, this is no time for fooling.

TEMPLE hangs up the receiver and turns to STEVE.

TEMPLE: What a fuss and flutter!

STEVE: Who was it?

TEMPLE: Our old friend, Judy Grant.

On the words 'Judy Grant' Mrs Trevelyan freezes and her face becomes dead pale.

STEVE: Judy Grant?

TEMPLE: She's a dear. But she fusses.

TEMPLE gets up.

MRS TREVELYAN also rises.

TEMPLE: … Don't worry, Mrs Trevelyan, I'll do what I can. And now you've given me these –

TEMPLE holds up the papers.

TEMPLE: – I'm sure they'll tell the police what they want to know.

TREVELYAN: Oh, thank you, Mr Temple.

TEMPLE: Don't mention it. Steve, will you show Mrs Trevelyan out? I'll try and get on to Sir Graham straight away.

STEVE and MRS TREVELYAN go out of the door as TEMPLE turns to the telephone.

But instead of picking up the receiver, he lays down the notes MRS TREVELYAN gave him on the table and taking from his pocket the slip of paper which he picked up in her room, he proceeds to compare the two carefully.

The slip of paper and the notes which start:

"Tuesday – 9.15 left Marshall House Terrace"

We see that the 'a' in the typewritten notes is in line and quite normal.

It is clear they were not typed on the same machine as the names on the slip of paper.

The type characters are in fact quite different.

STEVE hurries in and joins PAUL.

STEVE: Paul, my head's in a complete whirl. Is she the Girl in Grey?

TEMPLE: She's the Girl in Black now!

52

STEVE: But we saw the Girl in Grey ... out of the window. She came into this building.

TEMPLE: There are some sixty other flats, Steve.

STEVE: She behaved as if she knew nothing at all about that bomb.

TEMPLE: Perhaps she didn't.

STEVE: What?

TEMPLE: Anyway, this saved a journey to Wimpole Street.

TEMPLE holds up the notes and the slip of paper.

TEMPLE: This wasn't typed on Kohima's machine. The 'a' in these notes is normal. But she's made Canterbury more intriguing. Did you see her freeze up when I mentioned Judy Grant?

STEVE: I did. Actually, who was it ringing?

TEMPLE: Old Forbes. You should have heard him react when I called him a 'good girl'! Come on, let's get on the road. We've no time to lose.

STEVE: Don't forget we're using my car. And I don't want that smashed up, too.

TEMPLE: There's only one way to prevent it. Let me drive!

CUT TO: Canterbury Location. Day.

Shooting up the High Street, outside the City walls, with the West Gate in the background.

The sign on the Falstaff Inn is on the left background, STEVE's car with TEMPLE driving comes in from the back of the camera and pulls up sharply in the foreground.

STEVE: Stop! Here's the Falstaff!

TEMPLE: I know, sweet, only we want the Falcon!

STEVE: Sorry! (*She laughs and turns her gaze to the West Gate*) Oh, isn't that lovely – the Pilgrims Gate!

TEMPLE: No, darling – the West Gate!

They drive on through the old gateway into the Town.

CUT TO: The Inn Sign of The Falcon against its timbered roof and sky. Day.

CUT TO: The Falcon Hotel. The Hall and Reception Desk. Day.

The hall is stone-flagged, and the ceiling is supported by ancient beams.

The reception desk is, however, composed of modern partitioning with glass panels.

In one corner is the staircase, which turns on a half landing after four steps.

The door into the dining room leads off the half-landing. There is also a telephone booth in the hall.

Seated in a chair in one corner of the hall is a man reading a Kentish newspaper which hides his face.

TEMPLE, carrying a suitcase, and STEVE come into the hall and across to the reception desk, on which lies a visitors' book.

FRANK CHESTER is in the Reception Office and comes up to the desk.

He is a tough and surly looking individual, competent but without charm.

TEMPLE: Can you let me have a double room for myself and my wife?

CHESTER: How long for?

TEMPLE: Just the one night. We're sight-seeing.

CHESTER looks up his register.

CHESTER: That'll be all right. Number 10. Will you sign the book, please?

CHESTER pushes forward the visitors' book and TEMPLE signs for himself and STEVE.

CHESTER: Lunch is on now.

CHESTER points to the door on the half-landing.

CHESTER: That's the dining room.

TEMPLE: I'll just take the bag upstairs.

CHESTER: Leave it there. I'll take it up. You go to lunch.

TEMPLE: Thank you. Come on, Steve. I'm famished.

TEMPLE and STEVE start to go, then TEMPLE turns back.

TEMPLE: Oh, by the way, have you by any chance got a Miss Grant staying in the Hotel?

CHESTER: Grant? I don't think so.

CHESTER looks again at the register.

TEMPLE: She's an old friend. We haven't seen her for years. I heard the other day she was in Canterbury.

CHESTER: What initial?

TEMPLE: 'J'.

CHESTER: No, she's never been here.

TEMPLE: She's probably at one of the other hotels. Sorry to have bothered you.

TEMPLE and STEVE go through the Dining Room door.

TEMPLE taking his hat with him but leaving the bag.

The man reading the newspaper has lowered the paper and is looking after TEMPLE and STEVE.

From his position it is clear he must have overheard the conversation with CHESTER.

He rises and strolls across towards the desk where he inspects the entry in the visitors' book.

The man is WILFRED DAVIES whom we last met on the train.

CUT TO: The Falcon Hotel. Dining Room. Day.

The only feature of the room that concerns us is a big bow-window which juts right out over the stream.

In it stands a table laid for lunch, large enough for four people.

The normal backing is that depicting the ancient brick or stone wall of a building across the stream.

TEMPLE and STEVE are just sitting down at the table.

They look around.

STEVE: (*Pointing through the low window*) Isn't that attractive?

We see a view of the Stour from the West Gate Gardens through the window.

STEVE: Paul, you simply must take me on that river!

TEMPLE turns back and looks through the other side of the low window.

TEMPLE: O.K. but there's your contrast.

We see Greyfriars Monastery from the Garden seen through the window.

TEMPLE: As sinister as the other's attractive. That's the old Greyfriars Monastery where Richard Lovelace wrote "Stone walls do not a prison make …"

STEVE: "…nor iron bars a cage." Anyway, food first and then we'll explore.

STEVE picks up the menu.

TEMPLE looks at the spotless table appointments, silver, etc.

TEMPLE: Judging by the layout and the fact the waiter is obviously an Archbishop, we should do ourselves pretty proud. What's on?

STEVE: Potage Chasseur, Roast Lamb, Fried Plaice, Boiled Cod, Vegetables in Season, Apple Tart, Pudding Surprise, Vanilla Ices, Cheese and Biscuits, Coffee.

STEVE stops and stares at the menu.

The elderly and dignified WAITER obviously labouring under the secret sorrow that the service is not what it once was, now appears at the table and takes the menu from STEVE.

WAITER: I regret, madame, that that no longer signifies.

56

STEVE: All we want is …

WAITER: I'm afraid it's off – austerity you know. There's
           a little boiled cod – and I believe some pudding
           surprise.

TEMPLE: Well, Surprise Pudding sounds intriguing.
           Bring us whatever's left.

STEVE: But, Paul, I want you to look at the menu!

WAITER: I'm afraid it would only tantalise the gentleman,
           madame. Of course, at one time the food at the
           Falcon was considered the best in Canterbury.

*Meanwhile STEVE has been making frantic signs to
TEMPLE.*

TEMPLE: I can take it. Let me wallow in what might have
           been while you dish up the cod.

Reluctantly, the WAITER hands over the menu.

WAITER: Had you been in a little earlier, or – however …

The WAITER trails off and exits.

TEMPLE: What's the idea, Steve?

STEVE: (*Excitedly*) Look at the 'a's'!

The menu card is in TEMPLE's hand.

We see that all the 'a's' are out of alignment.

TEMPLE: You're right. Steve, I believe we've struck gold.

STEVE: That'll have been typed in the office. I didn't
           like the look of that manager. I believe –

WILFRED DAVIES enters.

DAVIES: Excuse me!

TEMPLE and STEVE look up.

DAVIES comes up to the table.

DAVIES: This is a terrible intrusion, but I was in the hall
           when you arrived and when I saw in the visitors'
           book it was Mr and Mrs Paul Temple, I could
           not resist speaking to you.

TEMPLE: That's very flattering, Mr –?

DAVIES: Davies. Wilfred Davies. This is my card.

57

DAVIES hands his card to TEMPLE who glances at it and passes it on to STEVE.

DAVIES: I'm not trying to do business with you, Mr Temple. But I am such a fan of all your books it is a real thrill to meet you in the flesh.

TEMPLE: That's very kind of you.

DAVIES: Do you know Canterbury well?

TEMPLE: I've only been here once before.

DAVIES: It is a very interesting place. So much more happens here than people imagine.

The WAITER returns and puts down TEMPLE and STEVE's plates of watery-looking cod and a dish of tired potatoes and cabbage.

DAVIES: But I'm keeping you from your lunch.

TEMPLE: (*Looking at his plate*) I don't think I'm very hungry.

WAITER: If only you'd been here before the war, sir –

TEMPLE: I believe this cod was.

The WAITER leaves.

DAVIES: Perhaps we may meet for a chat later?

TEMPLE: I'd like to.

DAVIES: (*To STEVE*) See you presently, Mrs Temple.

DAVIES starts to go, then comes back.

DAVIES: There is just one thing. I believe I heard you enquiring from the manager about a Miss Grant –

TEMPLE and STEVE react.

DAVIES: Miss J Grant.

TEMPLE: (*Guardedly*) That's right.

DAVIES: May I ask her Christian name?

TEMPLE: Jane.

DAVIES: Then I can't help you. There was a Miss Grant, a manageress, who bought some of my kettles

on my last trip, and I'm hoping to get in touch
with her this time –

STEVE: What was her Christian name?

DAVIES: Miss Judy Grant – quite a different lady from
            your Miss Jane.

DAVIES nods and smiles at them and goes out of the room.

TEMPLE and STEVE stare after him.

*Directly DAVIES is out of the room, TEMPLE jumps up from
his chair.*

TEMPLE: Come on, Steve.

STEVE: Where to?

TEMPLE: I've a hunch it'll pay to keep an eye on Mr
            Davies.

STEVE: But our lunch?

TEMPLE: It isn't edible, anyway.

STEVE rises.

*Just as STEVE and TEMPLE are moving across the room the
WAITER appears carrying two plates of pudding.*

WAITER: Sir! Your Pudding surprise!

TEMPLE: Thank you. We've had it.

TEMPLE and STEVE leave the restaurant.

CUT TO: The Falcon Hotel. Reception. Day.

*STEVE and TEMPLE, who is carrying his hat, come out of
the restaurant onto the half-landing.*

*In the foreground, DAVIES is talking to another man,
ROGERS.*

*STEVE and TEMPLE stop short, STEVE pretending to
powder her nose to fill in time.*

DAVIES: Something rather interesting's happened. I'm
            going to stop here, so you'd better go out and do
            the other job, here's the key.

ROGERS: You want me to go inside?

DAVIES gives ROGERS a key.

DAVIES: Yes. Get me all the information you can.

ROGERS: O.K. – Now?

DAVIES: Now.

DAVIES turns away.

ROGERS exits quickly through the main doorway.

STEVE and TEMPLE come down the stairs and start to follow ROGERS.

DAVIES stops them.

DAVIES: I'm just reading The Monogram Murders, Mr Temple. I wonder if you'd be good enough to autograph it for me.

TEMPLE: (*In a hurry*) Of course – sometime. If you'll excuse me …

DAVIES: I have it here – on the seat – it won't take a moment.

DAVIES crosses to the back of the hall and gets the book.

TEMPLE: Blast! Slip out quickly, Steve, and see if you can spot him.

STEVE exits hurriedly.

CUT TO: West Gate Gardens. Day.

ROGERS crosses towards Westgate.

CUT TO: Outside The Croft. Day.

STEVE is peering round.

CUT TO: Westgate Bridge. Day.

ROGERS comes round the corner and crosses the bridge.

CUT TO: The Falcon Hotel. Entrance Hall. Day.

TEMPLE finishes signing DAVIES' book and hurriedly hands DAVIES back his pen.

TEMPLE: There we are. Now if you'll excuse me.

DAVIES: Thank you. Mr Temple – very nice of you.

TEMPLE hurriedly exits.
DAVIES smiles to himself.

CUT TO: Kings Bridge. Day.
ROGERS crosses past the Weavers House.

CUT TO: Outside The Croft. Day.
TEMPLE runs and joins STEVE.
STEVE: Come on, Paul – I know which way he went.

CUT TO: Mercery Lane. Day.
ROGERS enters and takes a notebook from his pocket, looks
at it and then crosses the High Street towards Christchurch.

CUT TO: Westgate Bridge. Day.
STEVE and TEMPLE pause for a moment in the centre of the
bridge to spot their man, then press on.

CUT TO: Christchurch Gate. Day.
ROGERS crosses the square from left to right.

CUT TO: Mercery Lane. Day.
TEMPLE and STEVE hurry and reach the pavement leading
to Christchurch Gate.

CUT TO: Blackfriars. Day.
ROGERS hurries in and after glancing round unlocks the iron
gate to get into the garden.
He goes inside and relocks the gate.
He crosses the garden and goes up the steps.

CUT TO: Blackfriars. Day.
TEMPLE and STEVE hurry in.
They look round.

TEMPLE:	He's dodged us.
STEVE:	I know he came round that corner.
TEMPLE:	I wonder what this place is.
STEVE:	It's as old as the hills.
TEMPLE:	He must have gone inside.

TEMPLE and STEVE move over to the gate.
They try the gate.
It is locked.
They turn as a MAN calls to them.

MAN:	It's not open to the public, sir.

The MAN joins TEMPLE and STEVE.

TEMPLE:	Sorry, I didn't know. What is this building, anyhow?
MAN:	The old Friars Monastery, sir. It used to be on view, but it's passed into private ownership. You can get a good view from the water though.
STEVE:	The water?
MAN:	Yes, Miss – there's a ferry runs from the Falcon Hotel – bob a head.
STEVE:	Thanks – I said we'd be going on the river!

CUT TO:	A Landing Stage. Day.

The ferry boat is just filling up.
A BOY and GIRL TOURIST take the two bow seats, the BOATMAN is centre, and TEMPLE and STEVE in the stern.
The boat moves off.

BOATMAN:	Shilling each, please.
TEMPLE:	Remind me to touch old Forbes for our expenses.

CUT TO:	The Ferry Boat approaching Weavers House. Day.
BOATMAN:	Here you see a bit of old Canterbury. The houses we are now approaching were built by the Walloon and Huguenot refugees who settled here at the time of religious persecution in the Netherlands and France.
GIRL TOURIST:	When would that be? 1940?
BOATMAN:	No, miss. About 1500. They introduced the industry of weaving – this is called the Weavers House and they used to wash their heels in the river.
BOY TOURIST:	Their heels? Nice and nifty for the bathing!
GIRL TOURIST:	Stop it, Bert.
BOATMAN:	Heels! And there never has been bathing here – it's dangerous. There's a weir a short way down.
GIRL TOURIST:	Ain't them gables gorgeous?
BOY TOURIST:	Clark Gables to you, gorgeous!

STEVE is looking upwards and then looks left.

STEVE:	Paul, look! Isn't that lovely!

The BOATMAN glances off.

They are looking at the Cathedral seen across the bomb damage.

BOATMAN:	It is, Miss. There you have a h'aspect of the Cathedral unseen for centuries – by courtesy of the late Adolf Hitler and his bombing.
TEMPLE:	They certainly knocked Canterbury about a bit.

BOATMAN: Yes, but look at the view they gave us –
                  and anyhow you can't destroy a place like
                  Canterbury – not its spirit.

The ferry is now in the Monastery Garden.

GIRL TOURIST: Coo – this is pretty. What's the old bell?

BOATMAN: This is the garden of the old Friars
                  Monastery – the Black Brethren as they
                  were called – founded about 1208. It is
                  recorded that the site of their Settlement
                  was granted to them by Archbishop
                  Stephen Langton. The part we are now
                  passing was the Refectory or Dining Hall.
                  The monastery is no longer open to the
                  public 'aving been bought by private
                  interests. This part of it is of interest as
                  legend has it that when the monks first
                  came here no one would grant them any
                  land on which to build, so they erected
                  their Monastery, above the stream itself
                  with the vaults of same beneath the
                  waters. We are now entering the old
                  Water Gate.

GIRL TOURIST: Creepy, ain't it?

CUT TO: The Water Gate of the Monastery. Day.

We see an ancient wooden door right on the water's level.

BOATMAN: … This ancient entrance has not of course
                  been used for centuries.

TEMPLE: (*In a whisper*) I wonder!

*We see that on one side of the Gate are scratches and marks
which argue differently.*

BOATMAN: And that's as far as we can go this way.

BOY TOURIST: I could go a lot further under here – it's as
                  good as the Ghost Train.

GIRL TOURIST:	Bert – behave!
BOY TOURIST:	Go on, Pop – take us in the darker bit – don't be stingy.
BOATMAN:	What d'you expect for a bob – to cross the Atlantic?

The BOATMAN digs his oar viciously into the water.

| CUT TO: | The Landing Stage. Falcon Hotel. Day. |

The BOATMAN gets the boat alongside and the passengers disembark.
TEMPLE and STEVE enter the hotel.

| CUT TO: | The Falcon Hotel. The Reception Office. Day. |

CHESTER is seated, speaking on the telephone.

| CHESTER: | (*On the phone*) Who d'you want … speak up! … Mr Temple? … He's out. |

CHESTER looks up.

| CHESTER: | … Wait a minute. |

| CUT TO: | The Falcon Hotel. The Hall. Day. |

TEMPLE and STEVE come in.

| STEVE: | Then there was the menu, and Jane and Judy! |

CHESTER enters from the office.

| CHESTER: | Oh, Mr Temple – you're wanted on the phone – in the box. |
| TEMPLE: | Right you are. Wait here, Steve. |

TEMPLE goes into the telephone booth and picks up the receiver.

| TEMPLE: | Hello … Temple, here … Who's that … Spider! |

For the duration of this conversation, we intercut between TEMPLE in the telephone booth and SPIDER WILLIAMS who is in an office hut on Carter's Wharf, Rotherhithe.

SPIDER: I got good news for you … I've found the bloke wot took that car …

TEMPLE: Good for you. Who was it?

SPIDER: Don't want to talk over the phone! Line might be tapped. Meet me here … Carter's Wharf, Rotherhithe … Ten tonight … he's coming along …

TEMPLE: You're sure it's the man? … All right … I'll be there … But d'you know his name?

SPIDER: You come and ask him yourself …

A hand gripping a knife comes into the picture and stabs SPIDER in the back.

With a gurgling grunt, SPIDER slumps forward.

The hand raises his arm and replaces the telephone receiver on the instrument before SPIDER's grip can relax.

We see a silver pencil lying on the floor.

TEMPLE: Hello … Spider … Hello …

TEMPLE recalls the Exchange.

TEMPLE: … Exchange? … I've been cut off … What? … They cleared the line? … All right. Never mind.

TEMPLE hangs up the receiver and comes out of the booth.

STEVE: Who was it?

TEMPLE: Spider.

STEVE: What did he want?

TEMPLE: He's found the man who took Kohima's car.

STEVE: That's the man I want to meet. Who is he?

TEMPLE: He wouldn't say over the phone in case the line was tapped.

At this moment, CHESTER hurries out of the office.

TEMPLE looks at him suspiciously as CHESTER goes into the dining room.

TEMPLE: I wonder if it was being tapped. Steve, I'm not happy about Spider. We've got to get back.

STEVE: Straight away?

TEMPLE: (*Pulling out his cigarette case*) Yes. I'll have to pull in Forbes on this. You get the car while I ring him up.

STEVE: O.K. Thank goodness we didn't bother to unpack.

STEVE goes out of the door while TEMPLE moves to the telephone booth.

He pauses a moment as CHESTER comes hurriedly back.

TEMPLE deliberately drops his cigarette case, and CHESTER picks it up for him.

TEMPLE takes it by the edges and, as soon as CHESTER has gone, carefully wraps it up in a clean handkerchief and puts it in his pocket.

CUT TO: SIR GRAHAM FORBES' Office. Scotland Yard. Night.

FORBES is holding the silver pencil.

CRANE and TEMPLE are with him.

FORBES: Initials C.K.

CRANE: I've got it – Charles Kohima.

FORBES: By gosh!

TEMPLE: Might be Coffee Kenya, C.K.'s their advertising slogan. Poor old Spider!

FORBES: We did all we could, Temple. I even issued firearms.

CRANE pulls out a gun.

CRANE: Never had a chance to use it. Lovely bit of work too. One of the new .303's. Shall I hand it in, sir?

FORBES: Not for the moment … This case is getting too hot. Don't you agree, Temple?

TEMPLE: That's for you to decide.

FORBES: Well, what's the next move?

TEMPLE: I know mine.

FORBES: Yes?

TEMPLE: Bed!

CUT TO: TEMPLE's Flat. The Bedroom. Day.

TEMPLE is in bed.

He is, however, sitting up and busily writing in pencil on a pad.

The door opens very gingerly and RIKKI's face appears round the edge of it.

He gazes anxiously at the bed.

TEMPLE: (*Without looking up*) Darling! Come and give me a kiss.

RIKKI looks even more anxious.

RIKKI: Are you delirious, Mr Temple?

TEMPLE looks up and glares at RIKKI.

TEMPLE: Oh! What do you want?

RIKKI comes into the room carrying a hot water bottle.

RIKKI: In case you have cold feet, Mr Temple.

TEMPLE: Take it away! And I never have cold feet. Get Mr Brent on the telephone.

RIKKI: I'm so sorry to report our line is out of order.

TEMPLE: Blast! Slip down to the porter's room and ring him from there. Ask him to meet Mrs Temple and me at the Pompadour for lunch. Say it's important.

RIKKI: Yes, Mr Temple.

RIKKI is just closing the door when TEMPLE calls –

TEMPLE: Rikki!

RIKKI pops back round the door.

RIKKI: You've changed your mind about this, Mr Temple?

RIKKI holds out the hot water bottle.

68

TEMPLE: Certainly not. Ask Mrs Temple if she'll come in here for a minute.

RIKKI: Yes, Mr Temple.

RIKKI goes out, leaving the door ajar.

TEMPLE concentrates on what he has been writing.

We see his notes:

CHESTER: *-Dour, unpleasant personality.*
About 5ft 8in dark.

DAVIES: *-Welsh. Small.*

STEVE comes in.

STEVE: How are you feeling, darling?

TEMPLE: Fine. Steve, that chap Davies – how would you describe him?

STEVE: Well … he was Welsh … and he wasn't tall … and –

STEVE hesitates.

TEMPLE: Was he dark or fair?

STEVE: Sort of nondescript.

TEMPLE: Actually, my mental picture of him is very hazy.

The front doorbell rings.

TEMPLE: You'd better see who that is, darling.

STEVE: Rikki'll answer the door.

TEMPLE: I've sent him down to ring up Leo and ask him to meet us for lunch at the Pompadour.

STEVE goes out of the room.

CUT TO: TEMPLE's Flat. The Hall. Day.

STEVE crosses to the front door, opens it and reveals WILFRED DAVIES.

DAVIES: Good morning, Mrs Temple. Is your husband at home?

STEVE: Yes.

DAVIES: I wonder if he'd see me for a minute.

STEVE: I think he'd like to. Come in.
DAVIES comes in.
STEVE shuts the door and leads DAVIES across to the bedroom.

CUT TO: TEMPLE's Flat. The Bedroom. Day.
STEVE comes in.
TEMPLE: Who is it?
STEVE: (*Meaningly*) Mr Davies.
DAVIES comes into the room.
STEVE crosses and enters the bathroom.
DAVIES: Good morning, Mr Temple. I hope that you are not ill?
TEMPLE: (*Writing feverishly as he keeps glancing at DAVIES*) About 5ft 6 inches. Dark. Receding hair.
DAVIES: I beg your pardon?
TEMPLE: Sorry, Mr Davies. I was just making some notes for my book.
DAVIES: I understand! I have often heard novelists do most of their work in bed.
TEMPLE: We're a strange breed. Tell me, Mr Davies, how did you find out where I lived?
DAVIES: Your suitcase was in the hall at the Falcon. You have a label on it, Mr Temple.
TEMPLE: I see. Quite the detective!
DAVIES: Just normally observant.
TEMPLE: And what do you want to see me about?
DAVIES pulls a small note from his pocket.
DAVIES: This. I was in the bar and pulled out what I thought was a pound note. Someone must have put it in my pocket.
TEMPLE takes the note and reads:

TEMPLE: "No matter what happens Mrs Trevelyan is not
            REX. REX is the girl in grey". H'm.
DAVIES: What on earth do you make of it?
TEMPLE: I think whoever wrote this knew you would take
            it either to myself or the police.
DAVIES: I see. But why put it in my pocket?
TEMPLE: Maybe they thought you spotted something on
            that train, Mr Davies. After all, you were in the
            next compartment when Esther Van Ralston was
            murdered.
DAVIES: Yes – yes – it was dreadful. And there's
            something else I must tell you, Mr Temple.
            Before you left the Falcon, I thought I saw
            someone tampering with your car.
TEMPLE: I don't understand.
DAVIES: Actually, I looked through the keyhole of the
            garage, and …

DAVIES is interrupted by a knock at the door and looks up.
The door opens and RIKKI comes in.

RIKKI: All is satisfactorily arranged, Mr Temple. Mr
            Brent will meet you …

RIKKI suddenly breaks off as he sees DAVIES.
He stares at him for a moment, then hurries up to him with
his hand outstretched.

RIKKI: Mr Cartwright! This is indeed a pleasure!

STEVE comes from the bathroom where she has been stalling
about folding towels, etc.

DAVIES: (*Nervously*) Cartwright? What are you talking
            about?
RIKKI: (*Beaming*) You remember me – Rikki?
DAVIES: I've never seen you before in my life.
RIKKI: But Mr Cartwright!
DAVIES: I'm not Cartwright. My name's Davies.
RIKKI: But … but … the Angel Hotel, Sunderland.

71

DAVIES: Never been there.

RIKKI: When I was billiard-marker and you made the record break.

DAVIES: (*Angrily*) I don't play billiards.

DAVIES turns to TEMPLE.

DAVIES: I'm afraid this must mean I have a double!

TEMPLE: I find this most intriguing. Do tell me –

DAVIES: I have never seen your servant before in my life. Now I mustn't disturb you any longer, Mr Temple.

TEMPLE: Please don't go, Mr Davies.

DAVIES: I must. I have business. Goodbye, Mrs Temple. It has been a pleasure.

RIKKI: I will see you out – Mr Cart –

DAVIES: No. No. I know the way, thank you.

DAVIES hurries out of the room.

A moment later we hear the front door close.

TEMPLE bursts out laughing.

RIKKI: I can assure you, Mr Temple –

TEMPLE: (*Interrupting RIKKI*) That, Rikki, was Mr Davies of the Quick-Boil Kettle Company.

RIKKI: He was Mr Cartwright in the Angel Hotel, Sunderland.

TEMPLE: That's as maybe. Anyhow, Rikki, you've done me a very good turn.

RIKKI: (*Beaming*) It's a pleasure, Mr Temple. Would you wish it that I should follow Mr Davies – Cartwright – and try to discover the truth about him?

TEMPLE: No thank you, Rikki. I prefer to handle this myself.

RIKKI exits.

STEVE: Was that note from REX?

TEMPLE: Not unless Davies is REX – he wrote it himself.

STEVE: How do you know?

TEMPLE: REX, darling, uses a typewriter. But he's a most original man, our Mr Davies – the car was in a lock-up, you know.

STEVE: Well?

TEMPLE: It's the first time I've met anyone capable of looking through the keyhole of a Yale lock. Come on, we'll be late for the Pompadour.

CUT TO: The Pompadour Club. Foyer. Day.

LEO BRENT is waiting by the swing doors which lead on to the main staircase, running down to the restaurant.

He is smoking a cigarette with various members and their parties as they go into lunch.

The band is playing in the restaurant and there is a buzz of conversation and vivacious movement.

TEMPLE and STEVE come in and BRENT greets them.

BRENT: Hello there, Temple!

TEMPLE: Good for you, Leo. For once you're punctual.

BRENT: Shall I sock him, Steve, or will you?

CUT TO: TEMPLE's Block of Flats. Day.

A taxi draws up and the GIRL IN GREY gets out and goes into the block.

CUT TO: The Landing Outside of TEMPLE's Flat. Day.

The GIRL IN GREY comes along the landing and rings on the bell of TEMPLE's flat.

She is back to camera.

There is a moment's pause, then the front door opens, disclosing RIKKI.

GIRL IN GREY: Can I speak to Mr Temple, please?

RIKKI: He is out to lunch.

GIRL IN GREY: I've got to see him. It's terribly urgent.

73

RIKKI: First, you talk to me. Step inside, please.
The GIRL IN GREY enters the flat and the door is shut.

CUT TO: The Pompadour Club. Restaurant. Day.
TEMPLE, STEVE and BRENT are sitting at a secluded table.
Coffee cups are on the table and they are smoking.
TEMPLE: You've got the hang of it, Leo?
BRENT: The short answer is you want me to hike off to
            the Falcon Hotel at Canterbury, get the low-
            down on a stinkadors named Chester, and try
            and date up a dame named Judy Grant.
TEMPLE: That's it. And keep an eye open in case Davies
            alias Cartwright returns. Ring up the flat with
            any news, however trivial.
BRENT: And you say there's a chance of a rough house?
TEMPLE: More than a chance.
BRENT: And it's urgent?
TEMPLE: Vitally urgent.
BRENT stubs out his cigarette and rises.
BRENT: It's O.K. by me. I'll get off straight away. So
            long, Steve. If my luck's in, I'll have socked that
            bozo by cocktail time.
BRENT moves away from the table and TEMPLE and STEVE
watch him leave the restaurant.
STEVE: I'm quite sorry for poor Mr Chester! I believe –
Suddenly STEVE breaks off and points down the room.
STEVE: Look, Paul!
LATHAM and KOHIMA are getting up from a table down the
room.
They make their way out of the restaurant.
TEMPLE: Looks as if Latham's nerves were bad again.
STEVE: Have you found out anything about Dr Kohima,
            Paul?

| TEMPLE: | Nothing very sinister – except that in addition to psychoanalysis he's an expert in hypnotism. |

| CUT TO: | The Pompadour Club. The Foyer. Day. |

Barring the entrance to the restaurant stands the MAITRE d'HOTEL, before whom RIKKI is almost dancing with impatience.

| RIKKI: | But I must see Mr Temple. It is urgent. It is immediate. |
| HEAD WAITER: | You can't disturb him. If you care to give me a message for him. |

LATHAM and KOHIMA come out from the restaurant and signal to the cloakroom attendant, who disappears to get their coats and hats.

They stand nearby, occasionally casting a glance at RIKKI and the MAITRE d'HOTEL.

RIKKI:	Tell him it is a lady … dressed in grey …
HEAD WAITER:	A lady dressed in grey?
RIKKI:	She is waiting at the flat. It is most important she sees him immediately.

The attendant returns with LATHAM and KOHIMA's hats and coats.

They put them on, tip him and leave.

HEAD WAITER:	And what is her name?
RIKKI:	Just say … the lady in grey.
HEAD WAITER:	(*Significantly*) Mr Temple is lunching with his wife.
RIKKI:	(*Dancing with impatience*) Yes, yes. But the lady in grey says she is what he needs … that is, that she wants him … I mean.

The MAITRE d'HOTEL cocks an eye at RIKKI.

| HEAD WAITER: | Wait here. |

The MAITRE d'HOTEL goes into the restaurant.

CUT TO: TEMPLE's Flat. The Lounge. Day.
*The GIRL IN GREY is walking up and down, evidently in a
state of extreme tension.*
She keeps looking at her watch.
*We do not see her face, although she is of the same height and
colouring as MRS TREVELYAN.*

CUT TO: The Pompadour Club. Foyer. Day.
*RIKKI is still standing outside the swing doors to the
restaurant.*
*The doors open and TEMPLE and STEVE hurry out followed
by the MAITRE d'HOTEL.*
TEMPLE: Now, Rikki, what is it?
RIKKI: Mr Temple, the lady in grey is waiting in the flat.
           She said she must see you. The telephone is out
           of order, so she begged me to come and fetch
           you back –
TEMPLE: And you left her there alone in the flat?
RIKKI: Quite alone, Mr Temple.
TEMPLE: You prize idiot. Come on, quick.
*TEMPLE, STEVE and RIKKI hurry towards the door to the
street.*

CUT TO: TEMPLE's Flat. Lounge. Day.
The GIRL IN GREY is back to camera.
*She is sitting at the writing desk on which stands her grey
handbag.*
She is just starting a note.
On it is written:
"Mr Temple,
In case anything should happen to prevent me seeing you –"
Her hand comes into picture and writes:
"this is to tell you that REX is –"
The front doorbell rings.

CUT TO: TEMPLE's Flat. The Hall. Day.

The GIRL IN GREY hurries out of the lounge, goes to the front door and throws it open.

There is no-one there.

Then from out of sight on the landing is heard a muffled report, and the GIRL IN GREY crumples up in a heap on the floor, as the door, released from her hand, slowly swings to.

CUT TO: The Street outside of the Pompadour Club. Day.

TEMPLE, STEVE and RIKKI hurry to STEVE's car, and get in.

TEMPLE starts the car, but immediately stops, jumps out and comes round to look at the front tyres both of which are flat. In one of them sticks a piece of broken glass.

TEMPLE: Broken glass! We'll have to get a taxi!

CUT TO: Outside TEMPLE's block of flats. Day.

A taxi draws up.

TEMPLE, STEVE and RIKKI get out, TEMPLE thrusts a coin in the driver's hand, and they rush in.

CUT TO: The Landing outside TEMPLE's Flat. Day.

TEMPLE, STEVE and RIKKI hurry along the landing.

They see the door is ajar.

TEMPLE: Did you shut the door when you came out, Rikki?

RIKKI: I did, Mr Temple.

TEMPLE: Stand round the corner, Steve.

STEVE moves back.

TEMPLE pushes open the door.

The flat is silent and empty – except for the crumpled body of the GIRL IN GREY lying in the hall.

STEVE: Oh!

TEMPLE: Come along in. Shut the door, Rikki.

CUT TO: TEMPLE's Flat. The Hall. Day.
RIKKI shuts the door.
They stand looking down at the body.
STEVE: (*Whispering*) Is she … Mrs Trevelyan?
TEMPLE kneels down and gently turns the woman's head towards the camera.
We see that she is not MRS TREVELYAN.
TEMPLE: No one we've ever seen.
They all stare at the body in silence.
Then from off-screen is heard the sound of running water from the bathroom.
They look up.
The noise continues.
STEVE: (*Whispering*) There's someone in the bathroom
           – whoever did it is still here.

CUT TO: TEMPLE's Flat. Outside the Bathroom. Day.
TEMPLE enters from the hall and stands flat against the wall by the bathroom door.
TEMPLE: Come out of there – with your hands up. I've got
           you covered. Come on – come out of there.
There is a pause.
The water noise stops.
The door opens and INSPECTOR CRANE is discovered drying his hands on a towel.
There is blood on it.
CRANE: You're like I was, Mr Temple – just too late!

CUT TO: SIR GRAHAM FORBES' Office. Scotland
           Yard. Day.
FORBES, TEMPLE and CRANE are gathered round the desk on which stands the GIRL IN GREY's handbag, the contents of which are spread on the desk.

FORBES: I asked Crane to go round and tell you we'd traced the fingerprints on that cigarette case of yours.

TEMPLE: You mean Chester's?

CRANE: Sir Graham means the Manager of the Falcon. He's no more Chester than the man in the moon. He's Richard Mulberry, three previous convictions, including robbery with violence.

TEMPLE: I see. So that's why you came to the flat.

CRANE: I was only there two or three minutes before you arrived. The door was ajar. I went in and the woman was lying crumpled up in the middle of the hall. I got some blood on my hands checking she was dead. I went to the bathroom, found the bullet in the door-jamb. And was just washing when you arrived.

There is a knock at the door.

FORBES: Come in.

A POLICE SERGEANT enters and lays a paper on FORBES' desk.

POLICE SERGEANT: Report on the bullet, sir.

FORBES: (*Picking up the paper*) Good!

The SERGEANT goes out.

FORBES: (*Looking at the paper*) A .303 new issue.

TEMPLE: (*Blandly*) In fact, fired from a gun identical with the one which you had in your pocket last night, Inspector.

FORBES: (*Astonished*) Good Lord!

CRANE: (*Angrily*) You're not suggesting I shot her, Mr Temple?

TEMPLE: I'm not suggesting anything. I'm merely stating a fact.

FORBES: It's absurd! It's unthinkable!

TEMPLE: If you remember, Sir Graham, it has happened before.

CRANE: I protest, sir. This is a direct accusation!

TEMPLE: Calm down, Inspector. Right at the beginning, you formed the theory that REX is Dr Kohima and Mrs Trevelyan combined. And finding that pencil with C.K. on it by Spider Williams' body has made you more convinced than ever. You ridicule there is anything phoney about Quick-Boil Kettle Davies, alias Cartwright. And you don't seem particularly interested in Chester alias Mulberry. I only wanted to point out that we can't afford to ignore anyone in this case – especially as the murders mount up.

FORBES: Quite right. But don't worry, Crane. You're a long way down on my list of suspects. What we've got to do now is try and identify the Girl in Grey.

FORBES starts looking through the articles which have been taken from the handbag.

CRANE joins him.

TEMPLE picks up the handbag itself.

FORBES: Apparently her name was Carol Reagan.

CRANE: That's right. I've ordered a check-up to try and trace her.

TEMPLE is closely examining the bag.

He feels round the lining.

FORBES: Beyond that, we've nothing to go on.

TEMPLE looks up.

TEMPLE: Got a penknife?

FORBES hands a knife to TEMPLE who rips open the lining of the bag and extracts a rather crumpled card.

He glances at it and hands it to FORBES.

CRANE peers at it over FORBES' shoulder.

The card says:
WALTER AYRTON
77a, Soho Square,
W.1.
CRANE: Ayrton!
FORBES: Do you know him?
CRANE: Not personally. But I know of him, sir. He's a
            private detective – a professional – not an
            amateur.
CRANE looks witheringly at TEMPLE.
TEMPLE: (*Smiling*) Why don't we all go and call on him
            now – if that's not too amateurish a suggestion.

CUT TO: A Corridor in a building in Soho Square. Day.
TEMPLE, FORBES and CRANE have just come from the lift.
They start down the corridor when TEMPLE suddenly stops
them dead in their tracks.
TEMPLE: (*Whispering*) Look! Davies!
From a second corridor half-way up on the right, DAVIES
appears and walks rapidly towards a corner.
He goes round it and a door is heard to close.
CRANE: He's going into Ayrton's office alright.
TEMPLE, FORBES and CRANE proceed along the corridor
turning the corner until they come to AYRTON's office.
There is another office next door to it.
FORBES: He's vanished!
TEMPLE: (*Pointing to the other office door*) That's where
            he's gone.
The sign on the other office door reads:
QUICK BOIL KETTLE CO. LTD.
CRANE: (*Laughing*) One in the eye for you, Mr Temple.
TEMPLE: All the same – it's interesting.
FORBES grunts and opens the door marked 'AYRTON'.

CUT TO: AYRTON's Office. Day.

It is a small outer office.

In the background is a door leading into the inner office.

At one side is a desk, with a typewriter on it.

Behind the desk sits AYRTON's secretary.

FORBES, TEMPLE and CRANE come into the room.

FORBES: Is Mr Ayrton in, please?

SECRETARY: I'm afraid not.

FORBES: My name's Sir Graham Forbes. I'm Deputy
               Commissioner   at   Scotland   Yard.   I
               particularly want to see Mr Ayrton.

Meanwhile, TEMPLE has been looking round the room.

*We see him suddenly concentrate on the door leading to the
inner office.*

*We see that it is just slightly ajar, but as we watch it, it very
slowly and silently shuts from the inside.*

SECRETARY: Mr Ayrton's out of town, sir.

FORBES: When d'you expect him back?

SECRETARY: He didn't say.

FORBES: Ask him to give me a ring the moment he gets
               back, will you?

SECRETARY: Certainly, sir.

FORBES turns to go, but TEMPLE stops him.

TEMPLE: One moment.

TEMPLE suddenly flings open the door of the inner office.

The others join him and look in.

CUT TO: AYRTON's Inner Office. Day.

Placidly seated in a chair is DR KOHIMA.

*He looks round nonchalantly towards TEMPLE, FORBES
and CRANE who advance into the room.*

TEMPLE: Hello, Doctor. This is a pleasant surprise.

KOHIMA: Good afternoon, Mr Temple.

TEMPLE: May I introduce Sir Graham Forbes, Deputy Commissioner at Scotland Yard, and Inspector Crane?

TEMPLE turns to FORBES and CRANE.

TEMPLE: This is Dr Kohima.

FORBES: That's very interesting. May I ask, Doctor, what you're doing here?

KOHIMA: (*Pleasantly and imperturbably*) Waiting to see Mr Ayrton, Sir Graham.

CRANE: But he's out of town.

KOHIMA: I'm hoping that he'll return.

FORBES: Dr Kohima, we're here on very important business.

KOHIMA: So am I, Sir Graham.

TEMPLE: The Girl in Grey has been murdered.

KOHIMA: I'm very distressed.

CRANE: Then you know who the Girl in Grey is?

KOHIMA: I only know that you apparently thought she was my secretary, Mrs Trevelyan. And as I left her alive and well twenty minutes ago, I must confess I'm relieved you were wrong.

FORBES: And that's all you've got to say to us?

KOHIMA: I'm afraid there's nothing else of interest I can say. Except to renew my apologies to Mr Temple for the erratic behaviour of my car the other evening.

CRANE: (*Suddenly*) Ever use a silver pencil, Dr Kohima?

KOHIMA: Yes.

CRANE: With your initials on?

KOHIMA: Yes. Is there anything unusual in that?

CRANE: Always carry it about with you?

KOHIMA: Yes.

CRANE: Can I see it?

Then to CRANE's complete discomfiture, KOHIMA produces his pencil.

FORBES looks at KOHIMA for a moment, then turns to CRANE.

FORBES: Come along, Crane. We'd better get back. Good afternoon, Doctor.

KOHIMA: Good afternoon. If there's anything I can do to help, please ring me. I'm in the telephone book.

CRANE grunts disgustedly and follows FORBES out.

TEMPLE: Did you enjoy your lunch?

KOHIMA: I did. I think the Pompadour provides the best food in London. I find it very useful.

TEMPLE: So do I, Doctor. Au revoir.

TEMPLE exits.

CUT TO: A Corridor in a building in Soho Square. Day.

FORBES and CRANE are waiting for TEMPLE who comes out of AYRTON's office, shutting the door behind him.

FORBES: (*Exploding*) This case is the very devil. I don't know whether I'm on my head or my heels.

TEMPLE: Seems to me it's straightening out, Forbes. So long!

TEMPLE moves rapidly away.

FORBES: Hoy, where are you going?

TEMPLE: Home to put on the Quick-Boil kettle for tea with Steve.

CUT TO: TEMPLE's Flat. The Hall. Day.

The front door is opened with a latchkey from outside.

TEMPLE comes in.

He takes off his hat and coat and then goes to the lounge door, opens it and stops in astonishment at what he sees.

CUT TO: TEMPLE's Flat. Lounge. Day.

TEMPLE enters and sees seated at the tea-table STEVE and LATHAM.

TEMPLE: Hello, Latham!

LATHAM is tense and overwrought.

He jumps to his feet.

LATHAM: Temple! Thank God you've come!

STEVE: Mr Latham is very anxious to talk to you, Paul.

LATHAM: Actually, Temple, it's a little matter of business
           – private business.

STEVE gets up.

STEVE: And on little matters of business three's a
           crowd! Plenty in the pot, Paul!

STEVE smiles at TEMPLE and LATHAM and goes out.

TEMPLE pours himself a cup of tea.

TEMPLE: Another cup of tea?

LATHAM: No, thanks. Temple, I'm in the most terrible
           trouble.

TEMPLE: I'm so sorry.

LATHAM: By the mid-day post I received this.

LATHAM pulls a piece of paper from his pocket and hands it to TEMPLE.

We see the letter in TEMPLE's hand.

The 'a's' in the typing are normal and not out of alignment.

TEMPLE: (*Reading*) "Mr Latham, Tonight at 8pm you will
           deposit in person a despatch case containing one
           thousand £1 notes, not numbered consecutively.
           You will take them to the vaults of the Old Friars
           Monastery, Canterbury – entering by the north
           door which will be open and leave the case on
           the Abbots tomb. You will then immediately
           leave the city. If you fail to obey these
           instructions, full details of what happened in
           Cairo in 1937 will be sent to the Police. REX."

TEMPLE looks up.

TEMPLE: So, Cairo in 1937 rings a bell?

LATHAM: I thought it was all dead and buried … forgotten, Mr Temple! I can't tell anyone about that – not even you. I'm too ashamed.

TEMPLE: Then you propose to pay up?

LATHAM: I drew the money from the bank this afternoon.

TEMPLE: It won't be the last demand, Latham.

LATHAM: I know.

TEMPLE: Then why have you come to me?

LATHAM: I hoped … I thought … perhaps you could suggest some way out.

TEMPLE: Are you prepared to put yourself in my hands entirely?

LATHAM: I trust you implicitly, Temple.

TEMPLE: I shall have to bring the police into it.

LATHAM: The police? But –

TEMPLE: But I'll guarantee they won't press for any information about Cairo. Also, that they'll ignore anything that REX may have to say about it.

LATHAM: You're sure they will?

TEMPLE: I can promise you that if we can identify REX, I can make any terms we like with the police.

LATHAM: (*Hesitating, then making up his mind*) Very well, Temple. I'll take you at your word.

TEMPLE turns away.

He goes to the telephone and starts dialling a number.

TEMPLE: (*As if to himself*) 08.00 pm The Old Friar's Monastery, Canterbury.

CUT TO: The Monastery, Water Gate. Night.

FORBES and TEMPLE, equipped with torches, are already inside and CRANE is helping another detective, ANDREWS, out of the boat.

The shimmer of water can be seen flickering on the far wall of the tunnel and a certain amount of moonlight throws the figures into silhouette.

The head of a fifth man – presumably in the punt – can be seen.

In the foreground a stone corridor runs down – the ground dropping away steeply.

It leads to a cross corridor running left to right.

Very faintly some organ music can be heard.

FORBES: (*Whispering*) Good job you spotted this Water Gate, Temple.

TEMPLE: Yes. REX won't expect us to use his back door.

CRANE: You come with us, Andrews – Benson, you stay in the boat and keep your eyes skinned.

TEMPLE: Come on.

The four men – using torches – come down the passage and turn right.

CUT TO: Monastery. Second Corridor. Night.

The men proceed down a second corridor and go off right.

The organ music continues giving a weird atmosphere to the scene.

CUT TO: Monastery Crypt. Night.

This is a low underground vault, surrounded by Norman arches, and having high up in one wall an iron barred window through which moonlight shows sufficiently to let us see our surroundings vaguely.

In the forefront are some tombs – the principal one bearing the recumbent figure of an Abbot and having a Latin inscription – now worn and crumbling – on its side.

There are two entrances to the Crypt – one in the left foreground which is reached from the corridor from the Watergate and has steps leading down to floor level, and the other (or landward) entrance being a heavy studded oak door in the right background.

This also is well above floor level and has steps leading down. In the left background is an old lever or wheel controlling a wooden sluice through which a trickle of water is creeping.

TEMPLE, FORBES, CRANE and ANDREWS appear from the Water Gate entrance and come to the foreground.

The organ music continues.

CRANE shines his torch round.

The spot of CRANE's torch comes to rest on the Abbot's Tomb.

CRANE: You cover that side, Andrews – I'll wait by the tomb.

TEMPLE: Sir Graham and I will watch the north door.

The men break up.

TEMPLE and FORBES crouch behind a pillar.

FORBES: Thought you said this place was closed. What's the organ music?

TEMPLE: It's from the Cathedral …

TEMPLE looks at his watch.

TEMPLE: … a minute to go.

CRANE is crouched by the tomb.

The organ music ceases.

There is a deadly, uncanny silence.

FORBES: I hope to Heaven Latham doesn't funk it.

TEMPLE: Ssh! There's his car.

Distantly the sound of a car drawing up and stopping is heard.

The car door bangs.

A moment later the boom of the "Big Harry" bell from the Cathedral commences to strike the hour.

TEMPLE and FORBES turn their heads and look towards the North door.

The landward door slowly opens and LATHAM, carrying an attaché case and torch, enters.

After a moment he descends the steps.

His shadow is grotesquely enlarged passing along the wall.

CRANE is crouched in the foreground.

LATHAM enters and puts his torch down on the top of the tomb.

He then puts the attaché case on the slab as well and opens it.

He is eerily lit by his torch.

He looks scared as he opens the case in which we are able to see the bundles of notes.

He closes the case, takes the torch and turns away.

Reflected light from LATHAM's torch passes across FORBES and TEMPLE's faces as LATHAM's footsteps are heard receding.

They follow him with their eyes.

LATHAM passes through the landward door which he closes behind him.

After a moment, the sound of LATHAM's car being started up and driven away is heard.

TEMPLE again glances at his watch.

He looks up, then suddenly clutches FORBES' arm and points.

Another shadow is creeping across it.

Faint footsteps can be heard.

CRANE too suddenly tenses as he hears the steps.

He slowly draws his revolver with his left hand.

A gloved and overcoated hand comes in, lifts the lid of the case, closes it and starts to remove it.

Suddenly, CRANE's right hand seizes the wrist.

CRANE: (*Shouting*) Andrews! Quick, I've got him!

CRANE is holding the figure who is back to the camera by the wrist.

ANDREWS leaps in and grabs the other arm.

TEMPLE and FORBES rush up from the background.

FORBES: Now, Mr Rex – let's see who you really are!

The beam of FORBES' torch suddenly flashes up to reveal the terrified face of MRS TREVELYAN.

CRANE: Didn't I always say it was Mrs Trevelyan?

CUT TO: SIR GRAHAM FORBES' Office. Scotland Yard. Night.

MRS TREVELYAN is sitting in a chair, with an expression of dumb, yet obstinate misery on her face.

In front of her stand FORBES and CRANE.

TEMPLE is sitting on the edge of the desk watching them.

FORBES: Now, listen, Mrs Trevelyan. We've caught you red-handed. You're only making things worse for yourself by refusing to speak.

MRS TREVELYAN does not reply.

CRANE: Come on. You may as well make a clean breast of it. If anything will help, that will.

TREVELYAN: (*Slowly*) I've told you, I've nothing to say.

FORBES: Are you REX?

MRS TREVELYAN does not reply.

CRANE: If you're not, how did you know Latham was leaving the money in Canterbury?

MRS TREVELYAN remains silent.

FORBES gives an exclamation of annoyance.

TEMPLE rises from the desk and comes to them.

90

TEMPLE:	Can I have a word with her?
FORBES:	Certainly.
TEMPLE:	Alone?

FORBES looks from TEMPLE to MRS TREVELYAN and back.

FORBES:	All right. But I'll be surprised if you're any more successful than we've been. Come on, Crane.

FORBES and CRANE go out of the door.

TEMPLE moves across and stands in front of MRS TREVELYAN who stares back at him silently.

CUT TO:	The Corridor outside SIR GRAHAM FORBES' Office. Night.

FORBES and CRANE come out.

CRANE:	I've got it – an idea, sir! Kohima's here – in the Yard. You agreed we should ask him round and question him a bit more about that pencil.
FORBES:	That's right.
CRANE:	Well, sir, don't you see –

CUT TO:	SIR GRAHAM FORBES' Office. Night.

TEMPLE is bending over MRS TREVELYAN and speaking very earnestly.

TEMPLE:	Don't you see your only chance is to trust me?

MRS TREVELYAN stares back at TEMPLE without speaking.

TEMPLE:	Everything's against you. You haven't got a hope – unless you tell me what I want to know.
TREVELYAN:	I've got nothing to tell you – or anyone.
TEMPLE:	Yes, you have. You're the only person alive who can clear up this whole terrible affair.

It's so simple, too – I want you to answer just a few simple questions.

MRS TREVELYAN stares back at TEMPLE.

TREVELYAN: What are they?

TEMPLE: The night I came to your house in Marshall House Terrace – when you were called away by a phone message –

TEMPLE is interrupted by the door opening.

He swings round and MRS TREVELYAN rises, her hands clutching her throat in horror.

Standing in the doorway is DR KOHIMA.

Behind him can be seen FORBES and CRANE.

KOHIMA: Barbara!

DR KOHIMA hurries forward.

As he reaches MRS TREVELYAN, he holds out his arms to her, but she pushes him away.

TREVELYAN: Go away, Charles! It's nothing to do with you. It's my fault, my fault only.

KOHIMA: Now, Barbara, please –

TREVELYAN: Go away!

KOHIMA swings round on FORBES.

KOHIMA: What is this? Why's Mrs Trevelyan here?

FORBES: You know that, Dr Kohima, as well as we do.

TREVELYAN: No, he doesn't. It's nothing to do with him. I'll confess. I'm REX.

FORBES and CRANE move forward, CRANE fumbling for a pencil and pad.

KOHIMA: Barbara!

TREVELYAN: Don't listen to him! It's only me. He doesn't know. I tell you, I'm REX – I alone!

CRANE: (*Scribbling hastily*) You admit you wrote that blackmailing letter to Latham?

TREVELYAN: I'll tell you everything.

KOHIMA: (*Very forcefully*) Stop it, Barbara!

KOHIMA catches MRS TREVELYAN by the shoulders and forces her back in the chair, then he leans over her.

He stares fixedly into her eyes.

KOHIMA: Look into my eyes, Barbara.

TREVELYAN: Don't listen to him! I tell you ... I'm the only one ... only one ...

KOHIMA: Quiet, Barbara ... relax ... keep looking into my eyes.

TREVELYAN: Don't ... listen ... to ... him ... it's only ...

MRS TREVELYAN's face dies away, and her eyes become blank and fixed.

KOHIMA: Relax ... Your will is fused with my will. You will do as I say ... You will not speak until I say you may speak.

FORBES comes up to KOHIMA and puts his hand on his shoulder and pulls him away.

FORBES: What are you doing?

KOHIMA: Attending professionally to a patient.

CRANE: She's in no need of medical attention. She's agreed to talk and now I'm going to ask her some questions. Now, Mrs Trevelyan, did you write that letter to Latham?

MRS TREVELYAN sits motionless staring straight before her.

CRANE: How did you know Latham was going to Canterbury?

CRANE leans forward and turns back to FORBES with a puzzled expression.

TEMPLE slips forward and also looks at MRS TREVELYAN.

CRANE: She seems unconscious.

FORBES: Nonsense. Her eyes are open. She's only foxing.

TEMPLE: No, Forbes. She's in a hypnotic trance, isn't she,
            Doctor?

KOHIMA: Quite right, Mr Temple. Not another word will
            any of you gentlemen get out of her until I tell
            her to answer.

TEMPLE: And when will you do that?

KOHIMA: When I have Sir Graham's solemn assurance
            that she – and I – are free of all suspicion.
            Goodnight, gentlemen.

*KOHIMA moves towards the door but CRANE springs in
front of him.*

CRANE: No, you don't!

KOHIMA: (*Raising his eyebrows*) Am I under arrest?

FORBES: Now be reasonable, Dr Kohima.

KOHIMA: It's for you to be reasonable, Sir Graham. If I'm
            not under arrest, I'm free to go. If I am I demand
            to know on what charge.

TEMPLE: It's been a strenuous day, I think I'll get off now
            – with the Doctor.

*TEMPLE glances meaningly at FORBES, who reluctantly
motions CRANE to move aside.*

TEMPLE: See you tomorrow, Sir Graham.

TEMPLE and KOHIMA go out.

*FORBES and CRANE look at each other, then at MRS
TREVELYAN, sitting motionless with staring expressionless
eyes.*

FORBES: (*Exploding*) This is all darn nonsense. Get the
            police surgeon.

CRANE springs to the telephone.

CUT TO: TEMPLE's Flat. The Hall. Night.

*TEMPLE enters through the front door, shutting it behind
him.*

He looks at his watch – it is 10 o'clock.

94

He takes off his hat and coat.

TEMPLE: (*Calling*) Steve. Steve!

The kitchen door opens and RIKKI hurries out.

RIKKI: At last, Mr Temple! Mrs Temple has gone.

TEMPLE: Gone? What d'you mean?

RIKKI: At five minutes past eight she took her car to drive to Canterbury, as requested on the telephone by Mr Brent.

TEMPLE: Did she leave any message for me?

RIKKI: I was to tell you it was to meet Miss J Grant at the Old Friars.

TEMPLE: (*Frowning*) That's strange.

RIKKI: Mr Temple, I am unhappy in my mind about Mrs Temple.

TEMPLE: She'll be perfectly safe. Mr Brent'll look after her.

RIKKI: Something is wrong. I know it. I feel it in my bones. I have a hinch –

TEMPLE: A hinch? You mean a hunch. And you certainly will feel it in your bones if you don't get me some supper.

The front doorbell rings.

RIKKI goes to open it and discovers LEO BRENT who comes in.

BRENT: Sorry, Temple, I just couldn't take it any longer.

TEMPLE: Where've you come from?

BRENT: Canterbury. Of all the dead and alive holes, where the only thrill is when a knitting spinster drops a stitch –

TEMPLE: Where's Steve?

BRENT: I don't know.

TEMPLE: But your telephone message?

BRENT: I never telephoned.

RIKKI: I told you I had a hinch!

95

TEMPLE grabs his hat and coat, grips Brent by the arm and hurries him to the door.

TEMPLE: Come on.

BRENT: I don't get this. Where are we going?

TEMPLE: Back to Canterbury. Fast!

CUT TO: The Falcon Hotel. The Hall. Night.

A clock is striking midnight.

The only light is a single globe in the Reception Office, where the melancholy WAITER can be seen dozing.

We hear a loud knocking on the door. The WAITER stirs, gets up and shuffles across the hall and unbolts the front door.

Directly it is open, TEMPLE and BRENT hurry in.

WAITER: I regret, gentlemen, we have no rooms.

TEMPLE: Where's Mr Chester?

WAITER: He's not back, sir.

TEMPLE: Where's he gone?

WAITER: I couldn't say. He requested me to wait up for him. I've seen you before, I believe, sir.

TEMPLE: Did a lady arrive here about ten o'clock?

WAITER: I was in the dining room till well after ten. I'm sure I've seen you before.

TEMPLE ignores the WAITER and turns to BRENT.

TEMPLE: Listen, Leo. You wait here in case Chester returns.

BRENT: Where are you going?

TEMPLE: To the Monastery. If I'm not back in half-an-hour come after me.

BRENT: O.K.

WAITER: Now, gentlemen …

BRENT grips the WAITER.

BRENT: Shall I dot him one? – No, perhaps not.

TEMPLE hurries for the door.

WAITER: I remember! You're the gentleman who missed his Pudding Surprise.

CUT TO: The Landing Stage. Night.
TEMPLE gets into the boat and pushes off.

CUT TO: The Stream. Night.
TEMPLE rows along the stream which is dark and sinister in comparison with the occasional views of the Cathedral which is silvery grey in the moonlight.

CUT TO: The Monastery. Water Gate. Night.
TEMPLE's boat comes alongside.
He ties up the boat to an old iron ring.
Then he pulls a tyre lever from his pocket and manages to force the door open.
He steps inside, pulling out his torch.

CUT TO: A Narrow Passage. Night.
It is built inside the wall.
Steps lead down into the vaults.
TEMPLE goes down the steps shining his torch ahead.

CUT TO: The Second Corridor. Night.
TEMPLE goes through.

CUT TO: The Vaults. White Friars. Night.
The stone floor is wet and shining.
By the moonlight we see STEVE, gagged and bound to a pillar.
We see TEMPLE's torch approaching in the darkness.
STEVE's eyes light up with hope.
She struggles to make some sound.
TEMPLE sees her and hurries to her.

TEMPLE: Steve!

TEMPLE removes STEVE's gag.

TEMPLE: Darling, are you all right?

STEVE: Yes, Paul ... I knew you'd come ...

TEMPLE is just pulling out his knife to cut STEVE free when CHESTER steps from behind a pillar holding a gun with a coil of rope over his other arm.

CHESTER: We all knew he'd come. Stick 'em up, Temple.

TEMPLE swings round and seeing the gun slowly puts up his hands.

CHESTER: That was the whole idea! You've been getting altogether too nosey, Paul Temple, you and your wife. So now you're for it! Get against that pillar.

TEMPLE backs against the pillar to STEVE.

With his free hand CHESTER shakes loose the rope.

CUT TO: The Falcon Hotel. Night.

BRENT is standing over the WAITER who is cowering back in his chair.

The clock in the office shows it is 12.30.

BRENT: If I find you've moved when I get back, I'll sock you for six.

BRENT hurries to the door and goes out.

The terrified WAITER stares after him.

CUT TO: The Vaults. Night.

CHESTER has completed binding TEMPLE to the pillar opposite STEVE.

He stands back to survey his work.

CHESTER: I think that'll do.

CHESTER crosses to the side of the vaults, shining his torch ahead.

We see a rusty old iron lever.

He strains to pull it.

CHESTER: Can't wonder it's stiff. This old sluice hasn't been used for hundreds of years.

CHESTER manages to get the lever across.

We hear the sound of a gurgling inrush of water.

CHESTER: There! And now the water will fill the vaults and it'll be hundreds of years before anyone gets in here again.

Water is now pouring in through the sluice.

By the light of his torch, we see CHESTER climbing up the steps which lead to the passage and the water-gate.

At the top he looks back.

CHESTER: You'll have nice time to say goodbye to each other. I reckon it'll be some time yet before the water reaches the roof. And now I'll return your boat for you, Mr Temple.

CHESTER leaves.

The water is beginning to trickle across the floor.

STEVE: (*Panicking*) Paul, what are we going to do?

TEMPLE: Steady, Steve. We're going to be all right.

TEMPLE shouts at the top of his voice.

TEMPLE: Leo! Leo!

CUT TO: The Second Corridor. Night.

CHESTER moves along the corridor.

CUT TO: The Water Gate. Night.

BRENT heaves himself up just as CHESTER comes round the corner.

He starts to pull his gun, but BRENT leaps at him.

There is a brief struggle and then BRENT catches CHESTER an upper cut that knocks him straight into the river.

There is a splash.

BRENT: What the hell are you up to?

CHESTER struggles in the current of the water.

CUT TO: The Vaults. Night.
The water has now reached TEMPLE and STEVE's wrists.
TEMPLE: (*Desperately calling*) Leo!
TEMPLE and STEVE listen.
There is no answer.
STEVE: It's no good, Paul. We're done.
We hear BRENT's voice calling off-screen.
BRENT: Hello, there!
TEMPLE: (*Excitedly*) No, we're not! Leo! Leo!

CUT TO: The Second Corridor. Night.
BRENT hurries towards the vaults.

CUT TO: The Vaults. Night.
BRENT appears at the top of the steps and shines his torch on to the top of the water.
BRENT: Temple, where are you?
TEMPLE: (*Calling out*) Over here.
BRENT: Say, the place is afloat!
TEMPLE: You're telling me! Come quickly!
BRENT plunges into the water, holding his torch above his head.
TEMPLE and STEVE now have water up to their armpits. After a moment, BRENT, his torch above his head, swims in.
BRENT: I thought it was Cheltenham where you took the waters – not Canterbury.
STEVE: No – Bath.
BRENT: Bath is right.

CUT TO: The Falcon Hotel. The Hall. Night.
The WAITER is still sitting in the chair in which BRENT placed him.

We hear a loud knocking on the front door.
The WAITER hurries across and unbolts it.
FORBES and CRANE enter.

FORBES: Where's Mr Temple?

WAITER: Who?

CRANE: Mr Paul Temple.

WAITER: I've never heard of him, sir.

FORBES: (*To CRANE*) What the deuce do we do now?

CRANE: I'll contact the local police.

CRANE is just moving into the Reception Office to use the telephone when the door is flung open and TEMPLE and STEVE enter, followed by BRENT.
They are all soaking wet.

FORBES: Temple!

TEMPLE: How the Dickens did you get here, Sir Graham?

FORBES: Your servant rang me and refused to ring off until I promised to come down here. He seemed to think you were in danger.

TEMPLE: Rikki had a 'hinch' – and a right one. If it hadn't been for Leo here, our friend REX would have fixed Steve and me.

FORBES: REX! But how?

TEMPLE: Richard Mulberry, alias Frank Chester, tried to drown us.

FORBES: Where is he?

BRENT: Clogging up the weir, I'm afraid.

FORBES: Then at last we've finished with REX!

TEMPLE: Chester wasn't REX.

CRANE: (*Gaping*) Who was he, then?

TEMPLE: Judy Grant!

STEVE breaks into a violent fit of sneezing.

TEMPLE: Come on, darling. We must go and dry off. Coming, Leo?

TEMPLE starts to lead STEVE towards the stairs.

101

BRENT follows.

FORBES: (*Desperately*) But, Temple, one minute! If he wasn't REX, who is Heaven's name is?

TEMPLE: (*From the half-landing*) Only Mrs Trevelyan knows for certain.

FORBES: We can't get a word out of her. The police surgeon confirms it's a hypnotic trance.

TEMPLE: If you'll let me arrange things my own way, Forbes, I'll guarantee you shall meet REX face to face tomorrow night.

CUT TO: DR KOHIMA's Hall. Night.
The front door is opened from the outside with a latchkey and KOHIMA comes in.
He is looking anxious and worried.
He takes off his hat and coat and opens the door of his consulting room.

CUT TO: DR KOHIMA's Consulting Room. Night.
Kohima stands in the doorway and stops dead – his face registers surprise.
The room is in darkness, except for a pool of light thrown by a dark shaded reading lamp on to an armchair.
In the chair sits MRS TREVELYAN.
Her eyes are open, and she is staring fixedly before her – as we last saw her.
An expression of joy replaces KOHIMA's surprise as he hurries forward.

KOHIMA: Barbara! So those fools have come to their senses and sent you back …

MRS TREVELYAN neither speaks nor moves.

KOHIMA: … Barbara. It's Charles …

MRS TREVELYAN slowly nods her head.

KOHIMA: … It's all right now, you can talk now that I'm here.

TREVELYAN: (*Automatically*) Yes, Charles.

Suddenly the main lights of the room are switched on and KOHIMA swings round.

Standing by the light switch by the door is STEVE, whilst TEMPLE is standing close to KOHIMA, with FORBES on the other side.

Also in the room are CRANE, DAVIES and LATHAM.

TEMPLE: Thank you, Doctor. That is precisely what I wanted you to say.

KOHIMA: You've tricked me!

TEMPLE: You forced me to. Keep back, please.

TEMPLE crosses to MRS TREVELYAN.

TEMPLE: D'you know who it is talking to you, Mrs Trevelyan?

TREVELYAN: (*Speaking from within her trance*) Yes, Mr Temple.

TEMPLE: Will you answer any questions I ask you?

TREVELYAN: Yes, Mr Temple.

KOHIMA collapses in the chair behind the desk and buries his face in his hands.

TEMPLE: Stay by the door, Steve. In this room are assembled all the people – still alive – who have been connected with the REX case. And amongst them is – REX.

LATHAM: Re-REX is here!

LATHAM stutters slightly as he speaks and glances anxiously around the room.

DAVIES is staring at TEMPLE with the hint of a sardonic smile.

CRANE: (*Whispering*) You're telling me!

CRANE moves closer to KOHIMA who still has his head buried in his hands.

103

TEMPLE: There is one person who I believe possesses the vital clue, which will prove REX's identity. And that person is Mrs Trevelyan.

MRS TREVELYAN sits motionless, staring in front of her.

TEMPLE: I want all of you to remain still and quiet while I ask her a few questions. Put out the main lights, Steve.

STEVE switches out the main lights, so that the room is only lit by the pool of light from the reading lamp, which shines on MRS TREVELYAN.

The figures of the other people in the room can only be dimly distinguished.

TEMPLE comes into the pool of light opposite MRS TREVELYAN.

TEMPLE: Mrs Trevelyan, when were you first blackmailed by REX?

TREVELYAN: Nearly a year ago.

TEMPLE: Was it by letter?

TREVELYAN: No. He rang me up.

TEMPLE: Was it something to do with your past – or Dr Kohima's?

TREVELYAN: He threatened to expose Charles … for something that had happened in Egypt … years ago. Anything I did was to protect Charles.

TEMPLE: He knew you were in love with Dr Kohima?

TREVELYAN: Yes.

KOHIMA rises from the desk and is stepping forward when he is stopped by CRANE.

TEMPLE: Did REX ask you for money?

TREVELYAN: No. Just to send particulars of the case cards of some of Charles' patients.

TEMPLE: Why did he need them?

TREVELYAN: He was using the facts they had given Charles about their past to blackmail them.

TEMPLE: To whom did you send these records?

TREVELYAN: To Miss Judy Grant, Falcon Hotel, Canterbury.

TEMPLE: It was always women in whom he was interested?

TREVELYAN: Until he sent me to collect Mr Latham's money.

TEMPLE: Those instructions also came by telephone?

TREVELYAN: Yes.

TEMPLE: When you were caught, why did you try and take the blame?

TREVELYAN: If Charles knew I'd betrayed professional medical secrets he'd never have forgiven me.

TEMPLE: When you asked me to visit you at Marshall House Terrace, and were called away by telephone – was that also the same voice?

TREVELYAN: Yes.

A hand comes into frame and cautiously pulls out the top left-hand drawer.

TEMPLE: Can you identify that voice?

We see the revolver in the drawer.

The hand grips it.

TREVELYAN: I haven't been able to until tonight.

The hand gently lifts the revolver out of the drawer.

TEMPLE: Tonight?

TREVELYAN: I heard that voice speak in this room.

TEMPLE: And whose voice was it?

TREVELYAN: It had a slight stutter. It was –

We hear the sharp report of a revolver.

MRS TREVELYAN clutches her breast, half rises from her chair, struggles to speak, and then collapses in a heap on the

105

floor, knocking over the reading lamp, which goes out, leaving the room in darkness.
There is absolute silence, and we hear the banging of the door and the sound of the key turning in the lock.
Pandemonium breaks out.
TEMPLE: (*Shouting*) The lights! Steve! The lights!
The lights come on.
The noise dies down for a moment.
FORBES looks quickly round the room.
FORBES: My God! It's Latham.
Joined by CRANE, FORBES tries the door, but it is locked.
KOHIMA rushes forward and kneels beside MRS TREVELYAN.
TEMPLE is by the desk.
The drawer is still open.
TEMPLE: Your gadget, Doctor! He's locked himself in!

CUT TO: DR KOHIMA's Hall. Night.
LATHAM is struggling with the front door which is firmly shut.

CUT TO: DR KOHIMA's Consulting Room. Night.
FORBES and CRANE are still struggling with the door.
TEMPLE: You'll have to smash the lock!
TEMPLE turns to DAVIES who is close to him.
TEMPLE: Give 'em a hand, Ayrton!
CRANE: (*Incredulously*) Ayrton!
DAVIES: That's right. Carol Reagan was working for me.
FORBES: The Girl in Grey was working for you?
DAVIES: Certainly. Trying to get on to REX. Norma Rice's instructions. Let's try this.
DAVIES picks up a chair and starts bashing the door with it.

CUT TO: DR KOHIMA's Hall. Night.
LATHAM gives up his attempt on the front door.
The hall reverberates with the sound of the chair being bashed against the consulting room door.
LATHAM dashes up the stairs.

CUT TO: DR KOHIMA's Consulting Room. Night.
FORBES, CRANE and DAVIES are still trying to break down the door.
TEMPLE has drawn back the curtains, thrown open the window and is starting to climb out.
STEVE rushes up to him.
STEVE: Paul, what are you doing?
TEMPLE: There's a drainpipe. If I can get up to the first floor –
TEMPLE vanishes out of the window.
KOHIMA is kneeling beside MRS TREVELYAN on the floor with his arm under her head.
Her eyes open.
She is out of her trance.
TREVELYAN: Charles!
KOHIMA: Barbara! … Oh, my dear …
TREVELYAN: I'm sorry … please forgive me … I love you so, Charles!

CUT TO: The Back of KOHIMA's House. Night.
TEMPLE is climbing a drainpipe towards a small iron balcony onto which open French windows.
He reaches out with one hand, but the distance is too great.
He strains across.
He is holding the pipe with his left hand only – his grip being near a wall fitting.
The iron pins pull away from the brickwork under TEMPLE's weight.

TEMPLE leaps sideways as the pipe gives way.
TEMPLE grabs the balcony but succeeds in gripping it with one hand only.
He manages to bring his other hand onto the balcony and succeeds in heaving himself up.
He gets over the iron rail and kicks in the French windows. The glass shatters.

CUT TO: KOHIMA's Bedroom. Night.

Just as TEMPLE enters through the shattered French windows, LATHAM, holding his gun, flings open the bedroom door, being silhouetted by the light from the landing behind him.
TEMPLE leaps at him. He grabs LATHAM's gun wrist and after a struggle forces him to drop the gun to the floor and TEMPLE's foot kicks it under the bed.
We see it slither across the floor.
TEMPLE socks LATHAM hard and sends him sprawling across the bed.
On the bedside table is a bottle and glass on a tray.
LATHAM grabs the bottle by the neck and swings it at TEMPLE as he comes round the end of the bed.
TEMPLE ducks and falls. The bottle smashes on the end of the bed.
LATHAM leaps on TEMPLE.
The men roll over.
LATHAM tries to gash TEMPLE's face with the broken bottle.
TEMPLE strains his head away from the bottle.
He gives a convulsive heave and manages to get free.
They both rise and TEMPLE socks LATHAM again who smashes into the dressing table, dragging off the cover and contents and going down on one knee.

CUT TO: DR KOHIMA's Consulting Room. Night.
FORBES, CRANE and DAVIES are redoubling their efforts to break down the door which is now looking very shaky. STEVE is urging them on, half out of her mind with anxiety. KOHIMA is still attending to MRS TREVELYAN.

CUT TO: KOHIMA's Bedroom. Night.
TEMPLE and LATHAM are slugging each other. Suddenly, LATHAM lets fly with a terrific right and sends TEMPLE staggering back through the French windows. LATHAM leaps after him.

CUT TO: The Balcony. Night.
TEMPLE staggers out backwards and nearly goes over the guard.
LATHAM rushes out after him and tries to push him over.
TEMPLE's foot slips.
LATHAM pushes TEMPLE's head over the guard.
LATHAM: It's a long drop, Temple! This'll teach you!
TEMPLE suddenly gives a ju-jitsu twist which flings LATHAM aside.
TEMPLE: That's one Rikki taught me!

CUT TO: KOHIMA's Bedroom. Night.
TEMPLE and LATHAM rush back in from the balcony and slog each other some more.
TEMPLE is knocked towards the dressing table.
LATHAM picks up a chair and hurls it after him.
TEMPLE ducks as the chair hurtles in and shatters the dressing table mirror.

CUT TO: DR KOHIMA's Consulting Room.
DAVIES, FORBES and CRANE are still attacking the door.

CUT TO: KOHIMA's Bedroom. Night.
TEMPLE and LATHAM rush at each other.
First one goes down, then the other.
They clash, and LATHAM suddenly bends double causing TEMPLE to do a terrific fall right over him.
As he gets up LATHAM attacks again.
TEMPLE's face, already bloodstained, is battered by LATHAM's fists.

CUT TO: DR KOHIMA's Consulting Room.
CRANE, DAVIES, FORBES and STEVE are still battering at the splintered door which at last gives way. They rush out into the hall.

CUT TO: KOHIMA's House. The Hall. Night.
CRANE, DAVIES, FORBES and STEVE find themselves midway between the front door and the stairs.
They hesitate for a moment between the two.
After the battering on the consulting room door the house is strangely quiet.
Then from upstairs comes the sound of a single gunshot. The four react, then move in a body to the bottom of the stairs. Suddenly they stop and look up.

CUT TO: The Stairs. Night.
Round the landing at the top of the stairs comes a dishevelled figure holding a gun.
As it turns and comes a few steps down the flight we see that it is LATHAM. A look of horror comes over STEVE's face. Her hand flies to her mouth, half stifling her exclamation.
STEVE: O-oh!
LATHAM stops on the half landing.

LATHAM: Yes, Mrs Temple! Your husband's had it! And if there's any nonsense, you'll get it, too. Out of the way, all of you! I'm coming down!

LATHAM moves forward to the top stair.

Round the landing totters another figure – TEMPLE.

His face is bruised, his collar gone, his hair dishevelled.

He comes to the top stair, undetected by LATHAM.

Just as LATHAM is about to step off the half landing, TEMPLE gathers himself and leaps straight down onto LATHAM's back.

LATHAM falls, the gun flies out of his hand and lands at the feet of the group below.

TEMPLE is up first, and as LATHAM rises, TEMPLE measures him and catches him a terrific right hook.

LATHAM's head goes back, and he falls backwards down the stairs landing in a crumpled heap in the hall below.

CRANE and DAVIES bend down over the motionless body of LATHAM.

STEVE rushes up the stairs to where TEMPLE is swaying drunkenly on his feet.

STEVE throws her arms round him.

STEVE: Paul, darling!

TEMPLE: (*Trying to grin*) He was a rotten shot, Steve.

STEVE: Thank God, you're safe!

TEMPLE: But how right you were! No more crime for me, I'm sticking to novel writing.

STEVE: I know – until the next time they send for Paul Temple.

THE END

Press Pack

Press cuttings about three of the Paul Temple films ...

Send For Paul Temple

Thrilling and fast-paced action was again the highlight of the shooting last week on this new Butcher Empire film which John Argyle is making for F.W. Baker at Walton, with a big cast of box-office favourites, packing it with all the thrills, mystery, humour, excitement and suspense of the famous BBC serial, which has a record listening public.

The furious car chase filmed during the past week is said to be absolutely breath-taking in its speed and excitement. Down a long, and heavily tree-shadowed country lane at night, Paul Temple is driving with Joy Shelton playing a crime reporter, when he realises that another car is rapidly overtaking them at terrific speed.

His companion looks back, and realises that the car is being driven by one of the gang they are fighting, and that he is obviously trying desperately to overtake them. Suddenly Temple shouts, "Down, quick," – a shot rings out through the roar of the car engines, and – a bullet smashes through the windscreen. The crooks' car tears and then swerves furiously past Temple's and the collision is only averted by the driving skill of both.

Send For Paul Temple
More than three weeks of really hard work brought a well-earned rest over Easter to the team of technicians and artists working on the making of the film of the radio thriller which John Argyle is producing for F.W. Baker's Butcher Empire Group, with Joy Shelton, Jack Raine, Beatrice Varley, Hylton Allen, Tamara Dean, Michael Deacon, and a score of other well-known players.

Contented artistic and technical talent make for good film making, and John Argyle says that all those working with him deserve the highest praise for the material, technical and artistic results so far achieved, as evidence of which the rushes to date hallmark *Send For Paul Temple* as a front-rank production, an exciting mystery thriller, streamlined to a smash hit box-office formula.

Send For Paul Temple
Exciting mystery was the order of the day, and thrill followed thrill, as John Argyle continued shooting last week on *Send For Paul Temple*, which he is making for F.W. Baker at Walton, based on the popular BBC success by Francis Durbridge.

One of the most dramatic sequences had for its background an ages-old country inn, reproduced in fine detail, and with every exterior and interior angle available on one big set, thus eliminating any waste of time, and giving Argyle and Geoffrey Faithfull's cameras the widest possible scope, keeping the action moving at a cracking pace, so important in a mystery thriller.

The action moved from close-up forward through the bar, in front of the bar for a medium long shot, round to behind the bar, and throughout the whole charming old-world interior is in view, and through various alcoves and doorways can be seen the accessory rooms of the inn, giving complete depth to the scene. Once more George Paterson, the Art Director, and his team have done an outstanding job of set design and construction.

Paul Temple has been the principal player again, with such box-office favourites as Joy Shelton, Richard Shayne, Beatrice Varley, Hylton Allen and Phil Ray making up another fine team of artistes in important roles.

Midlands Show of Paul Temple

John Argyle, producer, and Francis Durbridge, author, of the Butcher Empire Production *Send For Paul Temple* will attend the Birmingham Trade Show at the Forum on Thursday, September 3rd, at 10.20.

The facts that they are both well-known natives of Staffordshire; that Paul Temple made his radio debut from Midland Region and that many of the scenes were shot in Staffordshire and Warwick gives this production strong local appeal. Nottingham exhibitors will also see it at Nottingham at the Elite on September 6th, at 10.45 a.m.

* * *

All have heard the radio voice of Paul Temple: the question now arises – who will play the part on the screen?

It is not an easy role to interpret, for the author, Francis Durbridge, who invented this character, has made him a modern person equipped with an up-to-date mentality and all

BUTCHER'S FILM SERVICE LIMITED
PRESENT

ANTHONY HULME
JOY SHELTON

Send for Paul Temple

Your Invitation

TRADE SHOW

FRIDAY, AUGUST 30th, 1946
at 2.30 p.m.

PALACE THEATRE, Cambridge Circus, W.C.

BUTCHER'S FILM SERVICE LTD.
175, Wardour Street, London, W.1.

No Children Admitted

Admit Two

BUTCHER'S FILM SERVICE LIMITED
PRESENT

ANTHONY HULME
JOY SHELTON

Send for Paul Temple

Your Invitation

PROVINCIAL TRADE SHOWS

NEWCASTLE—Grainger, Friday, August 30th, 10.30 a.m.
GLASGOW—La Scala, Tuesday, September 3rd, 10.45 a.m.
CARDIFF—Olympia, Tuesday, September 3rd, 10.45 a.m.
BIRMINGHAM—Forum, Tuesday, September 3rd, 10.30 a.m.
LIVERPOOL—Forum, Wednesday, September 4th, 10.45 a.m.
NOTTINGHAM—Elite, Friday, September 6th, 10.45 a.m.
MANCHESTER—Theatre Royal, Friday, September 6th, 10.45 a.m.
LEEDS—Tower, Tuesday, September 10th, 10.45 a.m.
SHEFFIELD—Union St. Picture Palace, Friday, September 13th, 10.30 a.m.

Head Office : 175, Wardour Street, London, W.1.

No Children Admitted

Admit Two

the advantages that advanced education and scientific knowledge can bestow. Well it needs them – for the twentieth century criminal is no Bill Sikes, relying solely on brute force to attain his ends. Therefore brawn must be pitted against brawn.

116

So the producers of *Send For Paul Temple* showing at the County Theatre, on Monday, for three days, were confronted with the task of selecting a Paul Temple, who would have an exacting job. They eventually picked Anthony Hulme as their man. He had just been demobilised from the RAF when production commenced.

Send For Paul Temple – Film Review
Detective melodrama. Crisp story, based on radio programme of the same title, of how novelist-detective rounds up gang of smash-and-grab raiders. Latter's actual operations somewhat gauche, and one poisoning sequence baffling in its implications of Scotland Yard and professional detective resource. Main narration nevertheless holding specimen of own popular type, complete with trio of murders, suicide, and mass of suspenseful business merging into well-knit melodramatic climax and eventful car chase and spectacular crash. Urbane title role characterisation, robust support, effective comedy relief. Reliable offering for detective-mystery devotees.

At one moment in this mainly colourful narration, a suspect is about to reveal the identity of the sinister Knave of Diamonds when he is handed a drink of cyanide, no less, in the presence of important Scotland Yard men. Here, one would say, is a first-class sensation which the humblest beat-pounder could not overlook – but no one takes the slightest notice of it, and even Paul Temple proceeds placidly to his next clue!

This sort of thing mars an otherwise plausible detective thriller in the Edgar Wallace manner. It is true that a couple of smash-and-grab raids are somewhat crude affairs, but in general there is very real suspense, drama and excitement in a citation of how novelist-sleuth Paul Temple rounds up the smash-and-grab raiders. A trio of forthright murders, a

117

determined suicide, and a mass of mysterious business involving shady characters using an inn as their hide-out – these are the assets which arrest the interest, and which merge into an eventful car chase culminating in a spectacular crash over a cliff.

For the devotee, then, here is quite an entertaining specimen of the detective-thriller species, effectively put over as to action and characterisation. In this latter regard, Anthony Hulme is suavely competent as the amateur sleuth, Joy Shelton supplies some feminine appeal as an alleged literary lady, and Jack Raine, Beatrice Varley and Michael Golden are particularly good in subsidiary roles. A word, too, for Charles Wade's comedy relief as a bland Oriental servant.

C.A.W.

Send For Paul Temple – A Review (contains spoilers)

Cut-to-pattern romantic crime melodrama based on Paul Temple, popular British radio detective. The jumbled plot, earnestly interpreted by an adequate rather than distinguished cast, doesn't follow the quickest route to its conventional "in the nick of time" ending, but, all the same, it succeeds in hitting a number of spectacular thrills as it enters the home stretch. "Penny blood" fiction faithfully picturised, it is, on the whole, good money's worth for provincial and industrial fans. Title values and the quota ticket are handsome additional measure. Honest British "thick-ear."

Story: Paul Temple, writer of best-sellers, is called in by Scotland Yard when a mysterious crime wave sweeps the country. Steve Trent, sister of a murdered inspector, collaborates with Temple and clues lead to a lonely country inn. Later, the innkeeper is bumped off, but still the identity of the leader of the vicious smash-and-grab gang that is causing the rumpus remains a secret. Miss Marchment, a middle-aged authority on inns, is constantly under the police's feet, but eventually she puts Temple on the right track. The showdown quickly follows and, believe it or not, the master crook turns out to be a Scotland Yard inspector! Temple and Steve find themselves in love.

Acting: Anthony Hulme is quietly effective as the keen and unruffled Temple, Joy Shelton wears a sweater with distinction as Steve, Beatrice Varley is responsible for a clever cameo as Miss Marchment, and Charles Wade earns a number of laughs as Rikki, Temple's faithful Chinese servant. Tamara Desni, Jack Raine and Hylton Allen also deserve a mention.

Production: The picture hasn't the scope, punch, nor the relentless drive of the average American thriller, but it is, nevertheless, acceptable stuff. There is the same far-flung and complicated tale – the villain hails from South Africa – spectacular penultimate punch, surprise climax and shy love interest. There is also the subtle warmth of our native heath. Couple these forthright attributes with good title values and the result is honest-to-goodness crime melodrama. Suitably exploited, it should easily get by in the suburbs, provinces and sticks.

Points of appeal: Popularity of thrillers, sound characterisation, English atmosphere, rousing climax and good title.

Meet The Screen Paul Temple by Herbert Harris
There are two Paul Temples – both busy getting their man.

One you only hear. He's the BBC version – Kim Peacock – occupied on *The Sullivan Case*. In this instance, Mrs Temple – "Steve" to millions of listeners – is Marjorie Westbury.

The other you see and hear. He's the film version – John Bentley – meeting the perils of *Calling Paul Temple* with guile and aplomb.

119

And his delightful missus "Steve" is here portrayed by Dinah Sheridan (actress wife of Jimmy Hanley and mother of Jennifer Jane and Jeremy James Hanley).

Author Francis Durbridge, whose pen consigns Paul Temple to the stickiest situations, but just as cleverly extricates him, is quite as busy as the sleuth himself – weaving a path between Broadcasting House and the film studios, with two desperate cases proceeding apace, and two Temples hot on the track. It's a heck of a time for the underworld.

Temple has become the Nick (Thin Man) Charles of the air, and Steve is Mrs Charles. The main difference is that Paul Temple is as vigorous as Nick Charles is languorous.

For those who like their whodunnits to have a body in every reel, *Calling Paul Temple* is their meat.

It has five murders. All the victims are wealthy women. Except for the word "Rex" chalked up near each crime, there are few clues. But Paul – with Steve's help – gets the killer in the end.

Fifteen well-known British male screen actors were considered for the part of Paul Temple, before John Bentley was chosen. Quite aptly, he has close connections with radio.

In appearance he is quite reminiscent of James Mason, but if you want to make Bentley really annoyed just describe him as "another Mason".

"Much as I admire Jimmy Mason," says John Bentley, "I do not want to look like him, nor act like him, nor in any other way try to resemble him. Let me be myself. Let me get ahead on my own merits!"

John was born in Birmingham thirty-one years ago. Oddly enough, the author of Paul Temple, Francis Durbridge, is also from Birmingham and has known John for many years.

Yet this in no way influenced the final choice of John for the part. Ernest Roy, producer of the screen Paul Temple,

"SEND FOR PAUL TEMPLE"

suggested Bentley for the part, and Roy only had his way after lengthy consultations with Durbridge and the director, Maclean Rogers.

Producer Ernest Roy had seen John Bentley in only one other film – Bentley's first and only film in fact – *Hills of Donegal*, but his work in that picture convinced Roy that Bentley had a future in British movies. I second that.

121

Before he left Birmingham Grammar School, John wanted to be a radio announcer. He had always wanted to be a radio announcer.

The officials at the Midlands studios of the BBC are not unaccustomed to people who turn up and say they want to be announcers.

They are not quite so used to applicants who turn up, as John did, still wearing his school cap and blazer. Perhaps this is why no less a personage than the BBC's Martyn Webster made it possible for John to realise his youthful ambition.

Soon after that he transferred his allegiance to Radio Luxembourg, whose programmes we used to turn to on Sundays for some light relief.

Within eighteen months he became Radio Luxembourg's chief announcer, the youngest in the station's history.

At the time, Durbridge was one of radio's youngest scriptwriters, but Paul Temple was not then even a gleam in the author's eye.

The two met at the BBC Midlands station and exchanged stories of their native Birmingham. Neither realised that more than a dozen years later John Bentley would be playing the lead role in the film of Durbridge's most popular radio character.

Bentley graduated from announcing to radio drama and had divided his time between this and the stage, his first London stage appearance being in the revue *New Faces*.

At the time of writing he has not yet been seen on the screen. His first picture, *Hills of Donegal*, has not been shown. John does not star in it.

Bentley plays opposite Dinah Sheridan, who is Mrs Paul Temple in John's second picture.

His new part is a great opportunity for John Bentley. It is impossible to estimate how many fans there are for the radio detective.

It goes into millions, not only in Britain, but in all the countries in Europe, where Paul Temple has become a national character in many different languages.

A number of different language versions of the film will be made for world distribution and John Bentley, Dinah Sheridan, Celia Lipton and Margaretta Scott will be heard by overseas filmgoers talking in a diversity of dubbed languages.

John lives near Leatherhead, in the Surrey countryside, devoting most of his time to walking, horse-riding and, in the summer, swimming.

It is a good thing that John is no weakling.

For his part as the stop at nothing, two-fisted Paul Temple, he has been trained by an ex-Commando for realistic fight scenes.

Picturegoer

Paul Temple Script Stolen
Thief Escapes on 'Borrowed' Cycle
A thief broke into the Walton-on-Thames home of film director Maclean Rogers, stole some jewellery and the script of the film *Calling Paul Temple* and then escaped on a bicycle, early to-day.

He broke into the house by breaking a kitchen window. "We heard nothing," Mr Maclean told me.

"We lost some jewellery, a gold watch, some money and the script. Luckily, the film is nearly completed and I had most of my notes about it at the studio."

After the thief ransacked the lower floors of the house, he broke into the garage and took a bicycle.

An Interview With Dinah Sheridan and John Bentley

On the set of the Nettlefold Studios, at Walton-on-Thames, I had a chat with attractive and vivacious Dinah Sheridan. It was a long time since we had met – she was playing in repertory in Wales at the time. I did not know then that there was a romance brewing; already Jimmy Hanley and Dinah had met whilst studying when they were quite young. "But we wanted to be quite sure about each other," she smiled. "Jimmy went off to the war, and I went into repertory; we both learnt a great deal about life during those years." The war over, Jimmy Hanley continued his brilliant screen career, and Dinah Sheridan became his wife, and she too was lured into films. "But my home comes first," she smiled. "We are very happy with our two children." All the same, Dinah is back in the studios as Mrs Paul Temple in the Nettlefold production, *Paul Temple and the Canterbury Case*. Ernest Roy is producing and Maclean Rogers directing.

"My sternest critic is my husband," Dinah told me, "but I love to have him in the studio when I am working, and when he takes a day off from his own filming he takes a busman's holiday and comes along to see how I am getting along. He gives me tremendous confidence."

John Bentley is co-starring in the picture with Dinah Sheridan. John reminds me slightly of James Mason. This thirty-year old Birmingham actor so far has only one film to his credit. Now he jumps to stardom. He told me that at first he was rather nervous in his approach to films, but everyone in the studios declares that he has a tremendous future. Tall and handsome, he is keen and unaffected. "I have no less than five murders to solve," he smiled, "with Dinah Sheridan to help me as Mrs Paul Temple." He was telling me that they went down to Canterbury for exterior filming. John Bentley has had considerable broadcasting and stage experience.

Seeing Double

Busy whodunnit specialist Francis Durbridge is having a confusing time these days. His day is divided between Broadcasting House, where his new serial, *Paul Temple and the Sullivan Mystery*, is under way, and the film studios where his *Paul Temple and the Canterbury Case* is being filmed.

So everyday he talks to two Paul Temples – at the BBC, Kim Peacock, and at the film studios, John Bentley. The rest of the cast also are, of course, duplicated.

In his spare time the Yorkshire-born Durbridge writes for the Press. He is the only radio writer to turn a radio serial into a novel. This was *Send For Paul Temple*.

New Cavalcade

Paul Temple and the Canterbury Case

Maclean Rogers has completed sequences featuring John Bentley, Dinah Sheridan, Margaretta Scott, Abraham Sofaer, Jack Raine and Ian Maclean, in Scotland Yard. Lighting cameraman Geoffrey Faithfull and operator Arthur Grant have filmed Abraham Sofaer in close-up whilst he hypnotises Margaretta Scott.

Dinah Sheridan is preparing for the scenes in which she will spend two full days in the studio tank. As Mrs Paul Temple she will be tied to a pillar in an underground vault which is then slowly flooded with water. To ensure that she does not have to stand in cold water, she has already been fitted with a frogman's suit which will not be visible in the film.

Author Francis Durbridge is a frequent visitor, dividing his time between Walton and Broadcasting House where his new serial is enjoying early success.

Paul Temple and the Canterbury Case

The interior of the Falcon Hotel at Canterbury occupies the smaller sound stage and here John Bentley, Dinah Sheridan and Hugh Pryse have been featured in sequences in which Mr and Mrs Paul Temple visit the hotel. Through the windows of the dining room there is a fine view of the cathedral.

Maclean Rogers and his stars return to the studios on Monday, after the Christmas holidays, and will start work on the big stage, where the crypt has been built, and where the studio tank will be utilised for water scenes. To ensure that John Bentley and Dinah Sheridan do not have to stand in cold water, hot air will be pumped through pipes into the tank.

Paul Temple and the Canterbury Case

This week Maclean Rogers moves his unit from the smaller to the big stage, to make use of the underground vault which has been erected. Master plasterer James O'Reilly had modelled his plaster and clay walls on a local church wall at Walton. With permission from the vicar he made a cast of a stone flint wall in the church, using this as his model, from which sections of wall were produced in jelly moulds. Tombs, with reclining knights in armour, and bishops, complete the illusion that part of historic Canterbury has moved to the studio.

The tank, which will be used for the sequences in which Paul Temple and his wife are held captive while water rises around them, has now been fitted with a warm air pipe, and is ready for use.

Paul Temple and the Canterbury Case

The interior of the vaults of the Blackfriars monastery at Canterbury has been rebuilt on the largest stage, where the flooding scenes are to be filmed.

Sound recordist Tommy Meyers is searching for the right "echo" to be heard in the vaults. His long experience of recording at Walton will soon give him the right answer.

Art Director Charles Gilbert visited Canterbury before returning to Walton to design the sets that represent the interiors of the historic buildings. Plasterers and carpenters are erecting some of the most convincing sets ever built.

Margaretta Scott and Abraham Sofaer have both completed sequences in Dr Kohima's flat. As Kohima, the mystery man of the story, Sofaer has been gaining the admiration of everyone in the unit.

Paul Temple – By Royal Command

Latest call for Paul Temple comes from Balmoral Castle. I hear that a British film dealing with the adventures of the BBC detective has been chosen for showing to the King and Queen and their guests.

Films shown in the Castle's private cinema are a frequent after-dinner entertainment at Balmoral. Pictures are chosen from lists submitted by British and American film companies.

The King and Queen and the Princesses are all film enthusiasts but they like to choose their pictures carefully. Personal taste in stars and stories govern their choices. So do film critics' reviews and the recommendations of friends.

Stars of *Calling Paul Temple* are Dinah Sheridan and newcomer John Bentley.

Apart from one or two seaside showings the film has not yet been seen by the public. It will be released in December.

Journey To Balmoral

Paul Temple has been called to Balmoral by the King and Queen. The celluloid version of the radio detective is travelling along Deeside to-day in circular metal tins and should be at the castle in time for presentation after dinner tonight to the Royal Family and their holiday guests.

When they sit down for the showing of the film – *Calling Paul Temple*, recently completed at Nettlefold – they are in for a night of adventure. There are five murders, a car chase and a bomb incident. Temple (John Bentley) and his wife (Dinah Sheridan) are all but drowned in a flooded vault.

They will not see, however, a scene in which a crook threatens Temple with a broken bottle. The censors asked for the scene to be deleted.

Temple Serial Coincides with London Releases

The next four weeks are to be "Paul Temple" weeks in the London area. Yesterday the famous detective returned to the air as the hero of the new BBC serial *Paul Temple and the Curzon Case*.

On Monday December 13 a large number of ABC cinemas in the North London district start playing Nettlefold's *Calling Paul Temple*. In connection with one playdate, at the Palace, Kensal Rise, John Bentley, the star of the film, will be opening the local Boy Scouts Xmas Fair this Saturday afternoon. The Kensal Rise district has been plastered with notices advertising the film, and all the Boy Scouts in the district have been drawing attention to the fact that Paul Temple will be opening their Fair two days before the film starts its run.

Monday December 20 sees the North London release of *Calling Paul Temple*, which goes South of the Thames during Boxing week.

128

In many situations in the provinces, where it has been playing on pre-release *Calling Paul Temple* has been doing exceptional business. Glasgow figures were exceptionally high, and at the Savoy, Brighton, where John Bentley made a personal appearance with the film, business was excellent.

Cinema Magazine

John McLaren Aids Paul Temple Again – Gets Boy Scouts To Promise

When John Bentley, the screen's Paul Temple, was prevented from making a personal appearance through influenza last Saturday, another star of the Nettlefold film *Calling Paul Temple* came to the rescue. Instead of Bentley, it was Canadian actor John McLaren who went to Kensal Rise to open a mammoth Scouts' Fair within a few yards of the Palace, where the film is showing all this week.

2,000 tickets had been sold for the event, and John McLaren was mobbed after he had declared the fair open and advised the crowded hall to see the picture at the Palace during the week. For two hours he signed autographs, making every recipient promise to do his best to pay a visit to the film.

Calling Paul Temple is playing at several other ABC cinemas in the Willesden-Kensal Rise-Harrow Road and Bayswater districts this week, and the Willesden Scouts Group, which is one of the largest in North London, has promised to round up every Paul Temple fan in the district to see the picture.

Paul Temple To Get Good Tie-Ups

A fortnight before the Christmas holiday general release of *Calling Paul Temple*, the popular radio detective returns to regular weekly broadcasting in a new Francis Durbridge serial entitled *Paul Temple and the Curzon Case*.

This marks the 10th year in the life of Paul Temple, and the BBC serial will undoubtedly do much to publicise the Paul Temple film, which is due to play Associated British cinemas on release.

An adaptation of the story of the film appears in the new Amalgamated Press *Boy's Cinema Annual*, just published. One of the most popular gifts for boys, it will be entirely sold out by the holidays, when the picture is released.

Cinema Magazine

Talking of Nettlefold films ... there's going to be a gay turn out of stars when *Calling Paul Temple* is trade shown at the Palace on Tuesday. John Bentley, Dinah Sheridan, Margaretta Scott, Abraham Sofaer and Celia Lipton will be there. Butcher's have also devised an exploitation campaign to tie-up with provincial trade shows and first play-dates. Which means that they have good reason to go all out on the film.

Incidentally, Ernest Roy is agreeing with the action of the Censor in eliminating a fight scene from the Paul Temple film ... a broken bottle is involved and the scene in which the crook raises the bottle to attack Paul Temple has been deleted ...

Says producer Ernest Roy ... "The Censor's cut is a wise one. In what we believe is a really exciting film, we have tried to avoid anything which might upset Paul Temple's millions of younger admirers" ... The film contains five murders, a car chase, a bomb incident, a poisoning, and shows Paul and Steve threatened with drowning in a flooded vault.

Paul Temple at Canterbury

The film, *Calling Paul Temple*, which will be showing at the Regal for six days from January 17th next year, has a very special attraction for residents in the Canterbury district.

Many of the scenes in the thrilling story of murders and attempted murders are set in the city, and there are lovely photographic views of the Cathedral, the Westgate Towers, the Black Friars, and several of the Canterbury streets. In one of the scenes there is depicted an exciting chase of a fugitive from St Margaret's Street into Mercery Lane, while in another, two of the characters, Paul and Steve, are nearly drowned in the vaults of the old monastery by Frank Chester, the sinister manager of the Falcon Hotel, Canterbury.

In the early stages of production, the film bore the title *Paul Temple and the Canterbury Case*, but this was shortened owing to its length.

A radio version of the Paul Temple series is at present being broadcast once a week.

Kentish Gazette and Canterbury Press

An old radio friend makes a satisfactory screen appearance in *Calling Paul Temple*, a whodunnit in which the identity of the villain is, as usual, skilfully masked in the complications of the plot. Victims this time are a number of wealthy women and the background is the attractive cathedral town of Canterbury. John Bentley and Dinah Sheridan as Temple and his inquisitive wife, Steve, should not disappoint followers of the radio serial, and the supporting cast is unusually good.

Calling Paul Temple – A Review (contains spoilers)
Murder mystery comedy melodrama, illustrating a hectic page from the casebook of Paul Temple, popular radio detective. A highly coloured mixture of blackmail, mayhem and murder, it records the grisly crimes and witnesses the spectacular end of a particularly cunning killer. The death rate is heavy, but luckily its sense of humour never deserts it. Modelled on *Thin Man* lines, it neatly punctuates its rough

stuff with jolly domestic asides. Good title thriller for the family and fans.

Story – A number of wealthy women are murdered, but the police are unable to get a line on the killer. Paul Temple, the famous author-criminologist, decides to have a crack at the case, and his wife, Steve, acts as his Dr Watson. Sir Graham Forbes, Deputy Commissioner of Scotland Yard, is compelled to collaborate. The principal suspects are a mysterious woman known as the "Girl in Grey"; Wilfred Davies, a commercial traveller; Dr Kohima, an Egyptian nerve specialist; Mrs Trevelyan, Kohima's secretary; and Edward Latham, a man about town.

After nearly coming to sticky ends in Canterbury, Paul and Steve manage to manoeuvre the suspects into Kohima's consulting room. Mrs Trevelyan, who knows more than she cares to tell, is then put into a trance, but before Paul can squeeze the truth out of her she is shot. The killer is Latham and the motive for his crime is made abundantly clear.

Acting – John Bentley and Dinah Sheridan work smoothly in double harness as Paul and Steve. Margaretta Scott, Abraham Sofaer and Alan Wheatley are effective as the principal suspects, and Jack Raine retains his dignity in trying circumstances as Sir Graham. The supporting players are equally consistent and competent.

Production – The picture is staged on a considerable scale and colourful night club scenes, complete with songs, pleasantly sung by Celia Lipton, picturesque Canterbury exteriors and friendly domestic interiors give effective contrast to its full-blooded crime sequences. Greater value than *Send For Paul Temple*, its parent film, it measures every thrill with a laugh yet retains an essential element of surprise. Good title values fully underwrite obvious box-office appeal success.

Points of Appeal – Exciting and amusing story, versatile team work, sly feminine angle, robust climax, good staging and box-office title.

Calling Paul Temple – A Review (contains spoilers)
Murder mystery melodrama. Adroitly confected story of how Paul Temple tracks down murderer of a number of wealthy women. Interest seized in opening sequence of mysterious killing in railway carriage, and maintained throughout in series of further murders committed as victim is about to reveal killer's identity, and in charmed life qualities of hero's sleuthing, Temple being involved in narrow escape from time-bomb, near-death by drowning when imprisoned in flooded vaults, and hectic fight with now cornered killer after exciting chase. Narration punched over with verve, completed with well-marked suspense and occasional spectacular action, with angles of mystery effectively emphasised. Animated direction, suitably dashing title-role portrayal, competent all-round support, touches of pleasant cabaret. Outstanding title attraction for legions of Paul Temple devotees.

This Nettlefold Films Production has done ample justice to the famous radio thriller, which comes to the screen with all that hearty surface action and adroitly confected suspense which the faithful fans demand. On this occasion the go-getting Paul is concerned with a series of mysterious murders committed by a certain Rex. This is an army of suspects, naturally, even including a Scotland Yard inspector engaged on the case but once again true-blue Temple wins through and nails his man in an exciting climax.

The development is an entertaining example of its own popular type, and with its powerful title appeal, the film must prove a money-spinner for the showman. In addition to the series of baffling murders, the bustling action also pivots on the charmed life of Temple, who narrowly escapes death from a time-bomb, and with his wife, is nearly drowned in an old monastery vault to which the killer has been lured. To add to the excitement and suspense, there is a number of occasions when a character is about to reveal the identity of Rex, only to be shot down in that very split second.

John Bentley portrays the celebrated Paul on suitably dashing lines, with Dinah Sheridan playing up with spirit as his ever-loving wife, Margaretta Scott making a powerful contribution to the prevailing suspense, Abraham Sofaer an excellent choice for sinister-looking suspect, and Jack Raine repeating his facile study in professional sleuthing. A brief but telling appearance is also made by Celia Lipton in sprightly cabaret song, prior to herself falling victim to the apparently ever-present Rex, this latter role efficiently registered by Alan Wheatley.

C.A.W.

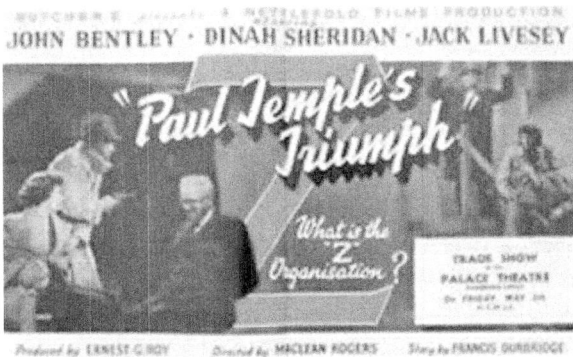

Paul Temple's Triumph – A Review

Crook melodrama. Neatly contrived story of Paul Temple's adventures in rounding up head of international gang out to secure British atomic secrets. Narration fashioned for action throughout, succeeds admirably. In forthright citation of

134

scientist's kidnapping, mysterious murder of daughter, use of dead man as booby trap, drugging of sleuth's wife by doctored cigarette, animated car chase which results in spectacular crash, and Temple's pose as gang leader which finally turns the trick. Unpretentious material punched over with vigour, readily achieving ambition of providing surface drama, suspense and thrill. Animated direction, enthusiastic portrayal. Safe offering for action devotees, with clear-cut title pull.

The popular radio sleuth, Paul Temple, has a job very much after his own heart in this Nettlefold production – he has to discover the headquarters of the dreaded "Z" organisation and arrest its leader. Knowing Temple as they do, his many fans will have no anxieties as to his ultimate success, but meanwhile Paul lives a charmed life indeed as he gets in and out of this and that tense situation.

Clearly, the development has no other pretensions than to prove lashings of action, and this it does from the word "Go" – the kidnapping, in other words, of a British professor engaged on an atomic invention. Things happen, all the time, when Temple gets on the job and discovers that the professor has been captured by the "Z" gang. Prominently, these dire events include the brutal murder of the scientist's daughter, the hue-and-cry to the New Forest, the discovery of a corpse which blows up when it is handled, the drugging of Temple's wife, the car crash of a woman member of the gang, and Temple's masquerade as the leader of the "Z" organisation.

All of which is punched over with zest and played with aplomb by a clearly enthusiastic cast. John Bentley dominates the proceedings with his incisive portrait of the sleuth, Dinah Sheridan is his ever-loving wife, and Jack Livesey a Scotland Yard man. The material cast also includes Beatrice Varley, Barbara Couper and Jenny Mathot, the latter the sadly victimised member of the gang.

C.A.W., News and Property Gazette

Paul Temple's Triumph – a review

Comedy crime melodrama, unfolded at a lively pace in a picturesque New Forest. Its story, taken from the casebook of Paul Temple, famous BBC detective, deals with the strange disappearance of a famous scientist engaged in important atomic research. Needless to say, an international spy ring is at the bottom of the trouble, and the cleaning up of the mystery makes full-blooded, disarmingly ingenuous "cops and robbers." How the kids will applaud its "U" certification! Good title thick-ear for masses and youngsters.

Story – When Professor Hardwick, inventor of a new atomic device, disappears, his daughter Celia contacts Paul Temple, the famous "private-eye." Sir Graham Forbes of Scotland Yard, and Temple are firm friends, and they decide to co-operate on the case. They are aware that a secret organisation known by the letter "Z" is operating in England, but before they can fully get into their stride, Celia and a plain-clothes man are bumped off. They then redouble their efforts, but they and Steve, Temple's wife, have many near squeaks by the time the professor is freed and the elusive head of the conspirators is unmasked.

Acting – John Bentley looks the part and acts with appropriate flourish as Paul Temple, and Dinah Sheridan is a natural and lady-like Steve, but Jack Livesey seldom relaxes as Sir Graham. The rest are so-so.

Production – The film leaves nothing to the imagination, but for those who like their characters labelled and their thrills underlined – and, judging from recent successes, they represent the vast majority of film fans – it's good money's worth. What it lacks in subtlety it more than makes up for in

136

vigour and pace. The kinema's equivalent to the bookstalls' penny blood, its market is both wide and certain.

Points of Appeal – Hearty action, popular light-relief, "nick-of-time" climax, quota ticket and box-office title.

Kinematograph Weekly

Where The 'Eyes' Have It by **Richard Pearson**
For the first time in entertainment history, the film studios in Britain are turning in a big way to the vast resources of radio material.

Current total on my local screen is as familiar as Friday – *Dick Barton – Special Agent*. At first sight it seems a ready-made box office success. The radio series with the same name is credited with ten million listeners every evening and if that isn't a pre-fabricated public for a screen play, I don't know what is.

Also showing round the country are the popular radio favourites William and Paul Temple, while coming along nicely are epics of Doctor Morelle and P.C. 49, among others.

But making film use of radio series is not a simple job of transferring story and characters to a new medium. Popularity on the air can be gauged only by counting ears – the listeners' only contact with the characters.

But on the screen it is the eyes which have to be satisfied for a character to find fame.

So the film producer's headache is to transform a voice into a complete body. With ten million critics waiting to say, "That isn't how I imagine Dick Barton!"

Well, how do you imagine Barton, or William, or Doctor Morelle?

Rarely, if ever, do we hear a description of these heroes on their radio series. They say things, we hear the results of their actions, but no one chips in a word about Barton's curly hair, or William's ears or the current ticklish problem of Dr Morelle's age.

Again, how would you imagine the supporting characters? Snowy is obviously light-haired and Cockney-born. But would you make him older than Barton, shorter, more humorous? And what of that irritating Miss Frayle? Is she in love with Morelle and, if so, doesn't that tend to make him a younger character than at first hearing?

It is not surprising that film producers, script writers and a selection of big shots go into bundles and generally disagree on points like these.

To their credit, in my opinion, they do their best to fit an actor to the part rather than just slam in a handy star under contract and let the public lump him. They also call in the author of the radio original and let him state his views of his character's appearance and idiosyncrasies.

On this point the Barton films get a big lift over the others for there is in existence a detailed "Life of Dick Barton" known to one and all as "The Barton Bible."

This reveals everything about this superman from the day of his birth. The day of the week – the job his father did – where young Dick went to school – and to college – his hobbies – wartime career – habits – and so on.

This is, I believe, the only life story of a fictional character ever written solely for behind-the-scenes use.

It was prepared originally as a guide to the radio script writers. If at any time they were not sure about anything Barton would do, such as smoke or take a drink, all they needed to do was consult the "bible".

Naturally, this is invaluable to the film director. It wins more than half the battle in presenting someone you know so well yet have never seen.

In the search for an actor to fit the exact requirements laid down, who should they light upon but Dick Barton's double in every way? His name is Don Stannard whose own life would match up well with the imaginary Barton. Athletic, world traveller, adventurer in queer corners, boxer, service man and film star, Don slipped into the Barton skin as if it had been made for him.

But still the film folk were not quite sure. So in early showings they staged personal appearances of Don along with the Barton film.

Just before the screening began, the doors opened, the audience heard a shout, a man ran down the aisle, and leapt dramatically on the stage.

Dick Barton stuff to a T.

Every audience took to Don at once. It was clear, then, that the film character was just what the radio listener had imagined.

A much more difficult task lies in putting over Doctor Morelle. The radio spot in which he appears is only seven minutes once a week. The film must be seventy minutes long.

Do you imagine Morelle as a lean, rather forbidding person? Or an elderly professor type? Much remains to be filled out about his appearance and character to spread seven minutes into seventy.

And some film experts doubt whether any picturegoer would stand seventy minutes of Miss Frayle as she sounds from her radio appearances.

Two queries I must clear up. Firstly, why can't the radio actors play the parts on the screen? Easily answered by the fact that few of them look like they sound.

Printed in Great Britain
by Amazon